The Master Of Frinton Park

by

Freda M. Long

Dales Large Print Books
Long Preston, North Yorkshire,
England.

British Library Cataloguing in Publication Data.

Long, Freda M.
The master of Frinton Park.

A catalogue record for this book is available from the British Library

ISBN 1-85389-672-1 pbk

First published in Great Britain by Robert Hale Ltd., 1977

Published in Large Print 1997 by arrangement with Robert Hale Ltd.

Dales Large Print is an imprint of
Library Magna Books Ltd.
Printed and bound in Great Britain by
T.J. International Ltd., Cornwall, PL28 8RW.

THE MASTER OF FRINTON PARK

Clarissa Branson married William Darker to please her parents. She started married life in total ignorance of the undercurrents swirling beneath the surface of life in her husband's fine house at Frinton Park. Why did Cousin Patience suffer the humiliations that went with the inferior status forced on her by the Darker family? And why was William in no hurry to protect his impoverished cousin when she was arrested for theft? With the shadows of the gallows hanging over the family, Clarissa took matters into her own hands—with baffling results...

1

Night Interlude

'Your skin feels like fine silk.'

She laughed softly. 'And yours like fine sand. You have made my cheek burn like fire.'

His mouth was close to her ear. 'What of the fire in your heart?'

'It burns so fiercely that I tremble lest it consume me.'

'*I* shall consume you. I shall eat you alive, tasty morsel by tasty morsel.'

'Love me, that is all I ask.'

'I do love you, my pretty bird. Have I not proved my love a thousand times?'

Her long-drawn-out sigh was a whisper of sound, lost in the louder sighing of the night breeze which fanned her hot cheeks, and lifted the carefully arranged curls on her forehead.

'Is it a proof of love to take a woman outside the blessing of the Church?'

'How many times must I counsel you to

have patience?'

'Often enough to make me wonder if you mean what you say.'

'Ah, you doubt my sworn word.'

'Only when you are not beside me.'

His silent, uncontrolled laughter affected her strangely. It was as if her words had motivated some hidden mechanism inside him, setting his body jerking in a sterile love-rhythm to which she could not respond.

'You must doubt a great deal then, since our days are necessarily spent apart.'

'Not for ever.'

'No, not for ever.'

'I love you.'

'And I love you.'

The mournful soughing of the wind in the trees, the mellow whistle of a curlew, wakeful in the full of the moon, the rustle of the undergrowth as prey fled from predator, his breath on her face, the all-encompassing blackness of ecstasy.

2

The Marriage Contract

It lay on her father's satinwood desk, white parchment and black, slanting copperplate, the marriage contract, with its shiny red seals and sleek green ribbons, its flamboyant signatures and its lawyer's jargon which made no sense to her...

'Whereas a marriage is agreed upon and intended with the permission of Almighty God soon to be had and solemnized between the said William Darker and Clarissa Branson, spinster, and whereas...'

Clarissa had fled from the library and the tyranny of those brand new parchments and seals, all those 'whereases' and 'wherefores', which tied her up as tight as a cat in a sack, to the peaceful confines of the orangery, a sad misnomer for a complicated glass structure, designed ostensibly for the cultivation of orange trees, but used more for social than for horticultural purposes, although Lady

Branson's geraniums flourished passably well there.

It being early April, the orangery was not presently in use, the ladies of the household deeming it an unprofitable exercise to walk a quarter of a mile over wet grass, followed by sullen servants bearing the silver and porcelain paraphernalia of rapidly cooling China tea, simply for the purpose of engaging in conversation. Tea and talk in the orangery were pastimes to be reserved for the more clement summer season.

In brief and welcome isolation then, Clarissa sat in one of the wicker chairs with a handkerchief applied to her nose—a precaution against the tangy, sneeze-provoking scent of her mother's potted plants—and her taffety skirts tucked up above her knees, disgracefully bow-backed as she studied her red leather shoes. The contrast between these hand-stitched beauties and her white silk stockings pleased her eye. She allowed her mind to meander down the pleasant path strewn with feminine gee-gaws which led her, inevitably, to form a mental picture of her bridal gown. Cream slipper satin sewn with seed pearls and trimmed with ruffles of Ghent lace, all to be worn over a tight laced corset and wickerwork pannier, the one to squeeze her to death, the other to make mighty certain that she fell flat on her face if she dared to move too quickly to the left or right.

When she was at last permitted to divest herself of all that cumbersome and expensive finery she would be a married woman, with her rights bartered away and the prospect of ten or fifteen years of child-bearing looming up before her. A baby a year for fifteen years if she did not die of exhaustion or milk fever after the first five or six.

Clarissa consoled herself with the thought that women had been known to suffer worse fates. Only last week a shepherd's wife had been hanged outside Lewes gaol for stealing one of her husband's flock, slaughtering it herself and salting the quartered carcase down against the unpredictable rigours of a Sussex winter.

At her trial the woman, with tears running down her cheeks, had begged the judge to have mercy on her. The previous winter one of her children had died of starvation. She had not been able to bear the thought of that happening again, so she had taken the sheep. The judge, unmoved by this appeal, had declared the prisoner to be 'an evil woman, firmly fixed in the ways of iniquity', and had sentenced her to death.

Clarissa remembered the exact details of the case, fully reported in the *Brighthelmstone Daily Courier,* because the name of the man she was to marry had been mentioned several times... 'Mr William Darker of Frinton Park, near Piddingfold, gave evidence against the prisoner, testifying that he had chanced to visit his shepherd's cottage while Mrs Dagg was in the act of sealing down her brine barrels, whereupon the unhappy wretch had broken down and confessed to her wicked crime...'

Clarissa leaned back in the chair, a pale, slender girl of twenty, with light blonde hair framing well-defined features, the austerity of which were wholly redeemed by large, luminous grey eyes, the latter imbued with a tendency to look inwards upon the pleasant, idle fantasies of her imagination. Deliberately, she conjured up an image of her betrothed. William Darker, thirty years old, a childless widower who lived with his two younger brothers, a sister and a distant female cousin. The sister, whom Clarissa heartily disliked, was described by the villagers as 'an ailing, skinny creature with the devil looking out of her eyes'. Mr Darker was tall and broad-shouldered, with steady, blue-grey eyes, a florid countenance and a firm, no-nonsense mouth. In sum, a stern-looking, uncompromising sort of fellow in Clarissa's opinion. His courtship of her had been brief and business-like, commencing exactly one year after the death of his first wife, when he had requested permission of Sir Charles Branson to call upon his daughter, and concluding six months later after a series of formal dinner-parties and less formal monthly assemblies held at the 'Blue Boar' inn in Piddingfold village.

Assembly nights had been the highlight of the month for Clarissa until Mr Darker's more than passing interest in her, combined with his unrelenting presence at the 'Blue Boar', had reduced her to a state of shrinking self-consciousness which completely destroyed her usual light-hearted enjoyment of the cotillions and other country dances.

It was such fun to squeeze into her father's barouche with her mother and sisters, to declare with a giggle that her hair was coming out of curl and her gown looked a fright, and to know, deep down inside her, that at least five or six gentlemen of the county would elbow each other aside in order to be 'particular' with her when the dancing was over.

When the overcrowded barouche rumbled to a halt in the inn yard, John, the family coachman, would jump down from the box and carry the ladies over the muddy cobbles, so that shoes and hems might not become soiled, depositing each fair burden upon the bottom step of the wooden staircase which led up to the improvised ballroom over the stables. The girls would skip lightly to the top of the stairs and wait impatiently for Mama's portly and breathless presence to join them before eagerly passing through the white-painted double doors, when they immediately became engulfed in the heat from the handsome fireplace, in which a great pile of logs always blazed away on assembly nights. Clustered about the fire would be the older ladies of the county, who were in the habit of arriving early in order to secure good places.

To Clarissa the scene had an ever-renewed enchantment; the gilt-framed, oval mirrors reflecting the crystal chandeliers and the high, brightly-coloured head ornaments of the ladies in an endless, diminishing perspective; the floor, well waxed with candle shavings and chalked in intricate patterns; the wreaths of evergreens slung along the cornice; the musicians sitting in one corner with harp, horns and fiddles; and all round the walls the rout seats for the ladies, young and old.

The evening invariably commenced with a minuet or two, in which the older folk would take the opportunity to display themselves, rising and sinking in Court bows and curtseys, while the young people waited and fretted with ill-concealed impatience for the country dances and cotillions to begin. The most important young ladies present, Clarissa and her two sisters among them, led off the chain in turn and called the figures, while the others ranged themselves down the room hoping for a long set with a favoured partner.

Every assembly night Clarissa, dutifully accepting her fate, performed two successive dances with Mr Darker and another later on in the evening. She could not have endured more, because Mr Darker was not the most light-footed of gentlemen and regularly ruined her slippers with his thumping gyrations. At all these entertainments he had complimented her on her 'glowing cheeks', or her 'lively spirits'—the two phrases, she had observed with wry amusement, being used in strict alternation—and had eyed her up and down with as much attention as he would have devoted to one of his brood mares. Indeed, on one particular occasion she had overheard a snatch of conversation between Mr Darker and Sir John Lambton, the latter an old friend of her father's, in which references were being made to 'a good breeder'. She had wondered at the time just who or what had been the subject of that exchange. She had confided these thoughts to the one person in her life who always told her the truth...

Sir Charles regarded his eldest daughter with quizzically raised eyebrows before saying bluntly, 'It is a consideration...when a man contemplates taking a wife, that is.'

Clarissa, always on easy, companionable terms with her father, made bold to ask, 'Has he offered for my hand yet?'

The paternal eyes crinkled into merriment. 'Not yet, but he is on the boil. I'll lay wager that he will beg leave to wait upon me within the week.'

'And you will signify your gracious consent to his request, take him into the library with a bottle of brandy and a pipe of tobacco, and behave in every respect as though you had not the least notion in the world why he had come.'

Sir Charles's huge frame shook with laughter. 'I daresay we shall sink a bottle or two.'

'While you arrange for the sale of one poor female.'

These words were not spoken entirely in jest, as Sir Charles was quick to perceive. His next remark was accompanied by a look of shrewd appraisal. 'Come on, Clarry, you don't want to fetch up an old maid.'

She remained stubbornly perverse. 'Aunt Charlotte is happy enough with her single status.'

This was too much for Sir Charles. He stuck his thumbs into the pockets of his striped silk waistcoat, wiggled his fingers at her and growled, 'Happy, is it? You think that chattering little mouse is happy, wandering from house to house like an Arab nomad, pitching her tent with any of her fond relations who grudgingly declare their willingness to put up with her...in return for her working like a blackamoor?'

Sir Charles sounded quite angry as he said this, and moved restlessly over to the old-fashioned Jacobean fireplace, where the cherrywood logs seemed reluctant to burn. One large booted foot kicked them into life and was slid craftily under a chair to wipe itself clean. He turned to find his daughter's wondering eyes upon him and chuckled briefly. 'Shocked you, have I, Clarry?'

She nodded, wide-eyed and a thought indignant. 'Indeed, Papa, you have. Aunt Charlotte is always made welcome in this house.'

His grey, slightly bloodshot eyes bulged into mock surprise, and the action of raising his eyebrows shifted his club-style wig a degree or two to the rear of his head. He adjusted it with a sharp tug, which now brought it too far forward, giving him the appearance of an inquisitive poodle.

'D'ye say so? Aye, now I think on it, I suppose she is. She is a dab hand at turning gowns and re-trimming bonnets for you girls when the seamstress is occupied elsewhere in the county, and she is good at waiting up too, till three or four in the morning, for thoughtless young things who have been enjoying themselves at assemblies and balls, and cannot wait to guzzle down more wine and fruit-cake when they come home...and there's none can make better cough syrup.'

Clarissa's cheeks became tinged with pink as she listened to this recital. 'Aunt Charlotte says she likes to make herself useful,' she ventured.

'So she may, poor creature. She is proud enough not to want to sit around all day existing on other people's charity, though it's always been a marvel to me that my food don't choke her. She manages to swallow it down, along with her pride.'

Sir Charles added for good measure, 'She's a deal worse off when she goes to stay with your Aunt Clara, I'll allow that. Now there is a woman for putting folk in their places. Charlotte is her sister too, thought you'd never know it, the way she carries on about dependent relatives, and how she herself follows the example of Our Lord by the giving of charity to others less fortunate, and how the milk of her human kindness flows over Aunt Charlotte.'

Suddenly, Sir Charles had taken pity on his discomfited daughter. He strode towards her and took her in his arms, crushing her cheek painfully against the gold buttons on his waistcoat. 'Have I painted the picture too harshly for you, sweetheart? I get carried away sometimes, just thinking of poor Charlotte. If it had been in my power when I was younger to find a husband for her I would have done so, but father always said she was too narrow in the hips to breed with safety, and he would not hear of her trotting in double harness. Fond of her, in his way, was father.'

Clarissa sniffed into her father's broad chest. 'Women and horses. Gentlemen have never been able to tell the difference, in my opinion.'

She extricated herself from the bear embrace as the deep rumble of laughter welled up in Sir Charles's chest and laughed with him, hands on hips, her head thrown back in the attitude which her mother so deplored. The candid amusement in her eyes struck an answering chord in her father's heart as she said, 'I see that I am well and truly hooked upon the prongs of the devil's pitchfork. Should I choose Mr Darker, with his horses, his dogs, and his guns, or should I choose to be like Aunt Charlotte, a hanger-on at the houses of my married relatives?'

She pondered this last point before asking with a smile, 'How would it be, Papa, if all three of your daughters were to remain single? Then we could live together, work at our tatting and patchwork, and go to church three times every Sunday.'

'Three female cats in a poke?' laughed Sir Charles. 'They won't draw well together, m'dear, you may take my word for it.'

The fire spat gold stars on to the deep-piled Turkish carpet, and the ormolu clock, with its flagrant cherubs, melodiously chimed the hour of the day...one...two... three...four. These homely, comfortable sounds, so achingly familiar, reminded Clarissa of what she was soon to lose—her home and the companionship of those whom she dearly loved. She said doubtfully, 'It is true that I do not find Mr Darker in any way objectionable,

Papa, though I fear he has little sense of humour.'

Sir Charles's face showed mild surprise, but he refrained from making the obvious rejoinder. He loved his children. He wanted them to be happy, a laudable desire tempered with sound common sense, and demanding that happiness be partially equated with a substantial fortune which he intended to procure for each of them in due time.

He had not been blessed with a son, a fact which he sometimes regretted but more often dismissed as irrelevant, one of life's little peculiarities. Lady Elizabeth Branson, his dear Lady Liz, fussed now and then over her inability to bear him a son and heir, but she knew that he attached no blame to her for her failure in this respect and loved him the more for it. Like most 'gentry marriages', theirs had been arranged by their respective parents, and it had turned out remarkably well. Sir Charles believed firmly in a father's right to choose husbands for his daughters. It stood to reason that an inexperienced female was ill-equipped mentally to select her partner for life. If he had left the business to Clarry, she would doubtless have picked

Sir John Lambton's scape-grace youngest son, that harum-scarum Harry, who was always running up debts for his father to pay. Handsome Harry, the girls hereabouts called him, and handsome he was, with his sea-blue eyes and his impudent, smiling mouth. He had stopped that before it had gone too far, no more than a couple of afternoon calls and holding hands on the rout seat at a village ball.

No harm done. Harry Lambton had a deal of fortune-making to do before he'd a right to take a wife. Frank now, his elder brother, would have done for Clarry. Only that saucy young miss from Steynford had hooked him good and proper with her dowry of one hundred thousand pounds, and not to be paid in instalments, either, as was customary. All in one lump—one hundred thousand pounds. It made a man's mouth water just to think about it. Mr Darker would have to make his peace with ten thousand pounds, paid in twenty-three monthly instalments of five hundred pounds over a period of five years, with interest at the rate of four per cent.

Darker hadn't haggled. You had to give him that. He had accepted the offer of ten thousand pounds without question, and had shaken hands on it too with a right pleasant smile. Sons. That was what Mr Darker wanted, more than all the money in the world. A man of thirty is getting past his prime. A pity about his first wife miscarrying and dying all in one. Still, it was good come out of evil, in a way. His Clarry would turn out sons by the dozen. He had a feeling. Everything was working out in a highly satisfactory manner. The wedding was being held just in time for him to see the knot tied before he went up to London for the summer session of Parliament. Finance Bills, wordy debates, and swopping yarns with the Duke of Grafton made a nice change from hunting and fishing. Foxes all looked alike. Well, damn him, so did politicians, come to that.

Sir Charles, permitting himself a snort of laughter at his own irreverent thoughts, was suddenly aware of his daughter's keen, intelligent eyes fixed enquiringly upon his face. He was seized by a strange feeling of tenderness. His Clarry about to marry, to become a wife and mother.

'Be happy, child,' he pleaded. 'Be happy with the man I have chosen for you.'

Impulsively, she ran to kiss his cheek,

saying confidently, 'I am sure I shall, Papa, since you have always cared for me so well.'

Devil take it, there was a lump in his throat as big as an egg. He swallowed painfully. 'Mr Darker is a good man, Clarry.'

Her eyes shone with merriment. 'And he farms a thousand acres and is worth six thousand pounds per annum.'

Sir Charles applied a large, lace-bordered handkerchief to his moist eyes, then blew his well-fleshed nose with a sound like a peacock's screech. 'Aye, so he has, which means, Miss Impertinence, that your widow's jointure will enable you to live in comfort in your old age. Thank the good Lord, Clarry, that ten thousand pounds was enough to fetch him.'

'Papa! Oh, Papa! I am not yet married and you speak of my days of wealthy widowhood!'

Sir Charles screwed up his face placatingly and flapped his handkerchief up and down. 'Ah, well, d'ye see, Clarry, there is the difference between men and women. We men take into consideration all possible eventualities, while the female of the species thinks of nothing but love and good looks, and does he pick his nose in public.'

Clarissa gave a little shiver. 'I trust that Mr Darker does not do anything so disgusting!'

Her father's grin was almost boyish. 'Not if that sister of his is with him. A prim little miss is Sophie Darker. I should persuade William to find a husband for her if I were you.'

Clarissa heaved a sigh. 'They say she is in poor health.'

'Mmm, well, it don't show when she's riding to hounds, which she does twice a week during the season. A feeling of fellowship with the deuced fox comes over me when I see her streaking away over Withy Down. The poor beast don't stand a chance.'

Clarissa dissolved into giggles. 'With Patience Pochin trying to keep up, and looking as miserable as a wet cat.'

This made Sir Charles frown. 'Aye...d'ye not think it strange that a girl of sixteen still has a keeper trailing at her heels like a pet lap-dog?'

'I suppose one would call her a companion,' Clarissa replied thoughtfully, 'although Mr Darker did tell me that Sophie is very young for her age and is still taking instruction. I understand Miss Pochin to be some sort of distant connection on Mr Darker's mother's side of the family. Her own family are in reduced circumstances, and Mr Darker has taken her into his household where she is regarded as something between a governess-companion and an upper servant. They call her 'cousin' Patience, but I have frequently observed Miss Darker using her with great discourtesy.'

'Miss Sophie is a pampered puss,' came the sharp rejoinder. 'Take my advice, Clarry, and get her married off as soon as may be.'

'Before I start meddling,' returned his daughter practically, 'I must get *myself* married.'

'I am looking forward to it, m'dear, if 'tis only to see your Aunt Charlotte with a ship on her head.'

Clarissa gave a little moan of dismay. 'Oh, Papa, she will not, will she? "Heads" look so out of place in the country.'

Sir Charles's high colour deepened to a reddish-purple as glorious recollections flooded his mind, recollections of his sister

Charlotte, dressed for an 'occasion', and having to sit on the floor of the coach to accommodate her 'head', which consisted of a Chinese pagoda hung with little bells, inside which a poor benighted goldfish swam round and round in a glass bowl. Then there was the time she set her feathers alight by bending too close to the fire and caused a stink which made everyone cough up their insides; and, best of all, the time when the wire cage supporting a magnificent erection of a bird in flight had snapped, and the bird had flopped down over Charlotte's nose.

'Perhaps we may allow her a very little ship,' he teased...

The sound of voices brought Clarissa back to the present with a start. Her mother's fluttery tones, at first only faintly audible, gradually increased in volume. 'How very kind of you to call, Mr Darker...I think that Clarissa...taking the air... One of the servants shall be sent to find her. I have been out walking myself, but I fear to take cold in this sharp wind...'

Clarissa, listening to Mr Darker's polite, agreeing noises, sighed deeply, squared her shoulders, and bravely broke cover.

3

Miss Sophie Darker Has A Pain

Dr Westlake, summoned with the usual degree of imperiousness to present himself at the Darker household, drove his gay little phaeton at a spanking pace round the sweep and reined in before the pillared portico of Frinton Park. The neat black mare lifted her head and shook herself vigorously, pricking up her ears as the sound of the physician's soothing voice commanded her to 'Whoa! Whoa there, Bessie. Gently, gently.'

Amidst this slight commotion the door of the house flew open and a small black boy bounded down the steps to perform his office of holding the mare's head. Red-satin suited, with a twist of silver turban wound round his woolly head, the child's appearance appealed to the physician's sense of the absurd. He could hardly hold back a chuckle as the little creature, eyes rolling with fright at the mare's antics, seized the bridle and led her at a slow walk towards the stable-court, there to await the return of her master.

The physician had not seen the child before and supposed that he had arrived with the last shipment of slaves from distant shores. Jamaica or Santo Domingo, was it not? Robert Westlake could not remember. He knew only that Mr Darker owned two slave-ships which provided a nice, profitable augmentation to his income from sheep-farming. The physician did not stop to consider the ethics of this trafficking in human flesh, though there were many in England in the year of Our Lord, 1768, who thought it wrong for any human soul, of whatever colour, race or creed, to be sold into bondage.

Bag in hand, the physician paused for a moment to admire the elegant façade of the house, the expanse of clean red brick, broken by long mullioned windows, and the imposing, Adam-style door, with its flanking pilasters and large fanlight. A carved stone label on the pedimented portico read, *Laborare est orare,* Mr Darker's family motto, a curious conceit since he did not bear arms. Directing his gaze heavenwards, Dr Westlake was charmed afresh by the guilloche string-course which ran along the edge of the roof like the icing on a wedding-cake.

The physician turned for a moment to survey the glades and valleys of the park which enclosed the house on three sides, and on the fourth stretched for half a mile beyond the formal garden, terminating in a wilderness of beech and chestnuts threaded with mossy paths. The brilliant colour of the turf was an unfailing temptation to Robert Westlake's eye, which seemed reluctant to detach itself from the luscious, emerald-green expanse and move on to embrace the line of sycamores, symmetrical as open parasols, and the huge beech spreading its fan on a seat placed round the bole.

Tearing himself away at last from the contemplation of so much grandeur, Dr Westlake took the steps two at a time and entered the house, reflecting as he did so that the black boy must enjoy extraordinary privileges to be allowed to use the front door for his comings and goings. The Darker establishment had been without a mistress for too long, that was very plain to see.

Miss Sophie's maid was waiting for the

physician in the hall and conducted him across the chequered floor, up the wide, open-string staircase, with its carved tread brackets and slender, turned balusters, and along a passage branching to the left towards the door of a bedroom which overlooked the formal garden at the rear of the house. The girl knocked lightly on the door before bobbing a curtsey and disappearing with a speed which suggested that Miss Sophie was not in the sunniest of moods.

The chamber which Dr Westlake now entered was decorated and furnished in the style known as Chinese Chippendale. Delicately limned birds of vari-coloured plumage flitted across the silken walls, while their counterparts, fashioned in thin porcelain, lined the shelves of a glass case, on nodding acquaintance with unglazed Dresden dogs, hunting stags and bears. The predominant background colour was pale green, a hue which did not please the physician's masculine eye, though he could not deny that the bed-hangings and curtains were of the finest sort, French silk threaded with silver and embroidered with wheat-ear garlands. The Turkish carpet reflected the pattern of the bed-hangings.

Apart from the bed, the room contained a Chippendale boudoir-table, a mahogany wash-stand and a rosewood chaise-longue upholstered in green silk.

Miss Sophie Darker reclined in careful disarray upon the chaise-longue, fully dressed in muslin and lace, and with her small feet encased in white satin slippers. Her left hand was placed with studied artistry across her flat bosom, and upon her face there was an expression denoting untold agony borne with truly Christian fortitude, but which seemed to the physician more a reflection of barely-concealed ill-temper.

After a conventional exchange of greetings, scarcely audible on the part of the patient, Dr Westlake was informed in feeble tones that a most disagreeable pain had occasioned this urgent summons to her bedside.

The physician bent over Miss Sophie's outstretched form with slightly more solicitude than he would have displayed towards his less affluent patients. He was a young man making his way in the world, and while perfectly in sympathy with any poor wretch who enlisted his aid at the price of four pence a visit, was not unaware that money and position were far more likely to be obtained through the good offices of the suffering gentry.

The action of placing the bell of his stethoscope against Sophie Darker's unblossoming breast, and of simultaneously lowering his head so that his right ear could be applied to the listening-piece, brought the physician's nose into closer juxtaposition than was entirely comfortable with a quantity of frilled lace, heavily scented with essence of lavender, which rose and fell in gentle sussurations of sound. He resisted the temptation to sniff.

Two minutes sufficed to determine the fact that Miss Sophie's heartbeats were astonishingly strong and regular. Straightening, the physician addressed her in calm, reassuring tones, noting as he did so the bright blush adorning her normally pale cheeks, and the engaging sparkle in her lively blue eyes. He said encouragingly, 'The pain of which you complain, Miss Darker, is not, I think, organic in origin. In my opinion it is occasioned by agitation, and a tendency on your part to become alarmed over trifles.'

It was perhaps fortunate that Dr Westlake

was not looking directly at Sophie as he delivered this diagnosis. Being in the process of bending over his black bag and replacing within its capacious depths the clumsy instrument he had used to gauge his patient's state of health, he remained happily ignorant of the fact that the fetching blush had receded somewhat from Miss Darker's cheeks, leaving in its wake two rouged patches which blazed like angry suns through a thick layer of white lead cosmetic paste, and that the eyes had lost their merry sparkle and now bored into his unsuspecting back like the killing beams of meteors.

Miss Darker very obviously did not approve of the physician's swift and unromantic summing-up of her parlous condition. For weeks now she had been the victim of a most mysterious pain in the region of her heart, a pain which could only be attributed to the stinging darts of love. Sophie had read a great deal about love. Knowledge of that ever-fascinating subject, culled from the pages of the novels of Mr Samuel Richardson and Mr Henry Fielding, was carefully stored in her brain, ready to be brought forth and applied when occasion demanded.

That her love for Dr Westlake went totally unrequited was all too painfully apparent to her, since he lavished upon her no languishing glances, nor yet permitted his hand to linger in hers a moment longer than was strictly necessary for the ordinary considerations of courtesy. His indifference made her angry.

He was turning now to look at her. She sat up, managing with remarkable agility to re-arrange her small features into lines of agreeable acceptance. He smiled at her. 'I shall prescribe for you a mixture of valerian and hiera picra to soothe your nerves, and perhaps a course of James's powders to purify the blood.' The smile grew broader, widening the straight gash of his large, full-lipped mouth to the point where it seemed his face must split in two. 'We must have you in fine fettle for the wedding.'

The warm, confident regard of the physician's restless brown eyes melted Sophie's legs and set up the irritating little churning sensation in her stomach which his presence so often engendered. Revelling in her self-inflicted martyrdom, she reflected sadly upon the unpredictability of unkind fate which had ordered

Robert Westlake's station in life, and placed him so far beneath her that to consider the possibility of his becoming her husband was quite out of the question. The idea, while it depressed, at the same time consoled, for it brought the added realisation that he would not so far presume as to think she might be interested in him as a man. What a simpleton she had been not to discern that his reluctance to declare himself sprang from a natural delicacy of feeling and a firm conviction that she would repel his advances with horror.

Sophie Darker, like most young women of her age, did not think beyond the present moment. It had not occurred to her that even had the physician forgotten himself sufficiently to respond to her naïve efforts at seduction, she would not have had the least notion how to handle such a potentially explosive situation. On the other hand, the fact that he did not, made her all the more determined to engage his interest, especially as she suspected that he was not oblivious to the quiet charm of Miss Patience Pochin.

Recollections of Patience brought with them a renewal of her anger, for she was too young and spoiled to contemplate the possibility of a rival in love with any degree of equanimity. Roundly, she declared, 'I hate weddings!'

The wide sweep of Dr Westlake's brow furrowed in amazement. 'I am astounded to hear you say so, Miss Darker. I am sure that you will revise your bad opinion of them when the time comes for *you* to enter into the state of matrimony.'

'That I shall never do, sir!' Sitting bolt upright on the chaise-longue, she refuted the suggestion with overdone petulance. Her intense, accusing stare caused him no little embarrassment. He had always considered her to be too distressingly vehement for comfort, a frustrated, tight little miss with too high an opinion of her own importance in the scheme of things. A word in the ear of Mr William Darker that he would do well to find his young sister a husband with all possible despatch might not go unheeded.

Robert Westlake was becoming distinctly bored with Sophie's desperate and distasteful attempts to flirt with him. He was too careful of his reputation to give her the slightest encouragement, but he greatly feared that an indiscretion on her part might reveal to William Darker the depth of her attachment to a mere physician. It was not to be borne that Miss Darker should be permitted to tarnish his good name.

It had taken him long enough, God knew, to establish his position among the Sussex gentry. The acquiring of a sickeningly servile bedside manner had been one of the first essentials, but that alone would have availed him little had it not been for the thorough grounding in medicine he had received under the great Dr Hunter at St Bartholomew's Hospital in London. Robert Westlake knew himself to be a good and competent physician, possessed of as much medical skill as his time could give him. One day, if he played his cards right, he would be as wealthy and as respected as Dr Hunter, and no love-starved little jade was going to thwart his very laudable ambition. Miss Sophie Darker, with her pale, heart-shaped face and her great, staring eyes, ignited no answering spark of love in his breast. To speak truth, her manner faintly alarmed him. He was certain that the pain of which she complained was self-induced, if not purely imaginary, and he had accordingly prescribed a placebo which could do her no harm and very little good.

Dr Westlake, now ready to depart to the humble abode of a more needy patient, an artisan whose broken leg was having to wait upon a young girl's silly vapours, smoothed the skirts of his black frock-coat, adjusted the snowy fall of white silk at his throat and offered Miss Darker a courteous bow. 'I shall come on Wednesday to see how you are progressing, Miss Darker, and if you have managed to swallow some of my witch's brew I fully expect to find you quite recovered.'

Sophie was annoyed that the physician had not chosen to pursue her interesting opinion upon the subject of marriage, which was based on nothing more solid than the fact that she loathed the natural corollary to such a union, to wit, babies, and all the fuss that attended their advent. She had secretly rejoiced at the untimely demise of her sister-in-law and her unborn child, experiencing a satisfaction only equalled by her dismay when her brother had announced his intention to re-marry. Daydreams of herself and her brothers, perpetually united, perpetually enjoying together the annual round of country-house entertainments in a state of youthful and suspended animation, faded into extinction.

Sophie acknowledged the physician's bow with a slight inclination of her head and said with obvious regret, 'No doubt your services will be required a great deal in the future, Dr Westlake, should my brother's bride prove fertile.'

He appeared a thought taken aback by such indelicate outspokenness upon a subject not generally discussed by well brought-up unmarried females. Alas, Miss Darker lacked a mother, and had no doubt heard her brothers speaking of matters not fit for the withdrawing-room. He said rather self-consciously, 'I pray most heartily I shall be often summoned on that account.' He added unwisely, 'Let us hope that the new Mrs Darker may be blessed with one or two little ones of the female gender. It may then be possible to persuade your most estimable Miss Pochin to stay on and teach them their letters.'

Sophie's light laugh was unfeignedly malicious. 'Sir, *my estimable Miss Pochin* has little choice but to remain with us. She is what is termed an indigent gentlewoman.' She added spitefully, 'Anyway, she will be in her dotage before your fictitious infants are ready to take instruction.'

The physician thought the remark not only spiteful but extremely unladylike, a fact to which his tightly indrawn lips testified. He said pointedly, 'Miss Pochin is not above five-and-twenty, I believe.'

Sophie's ruthlessly plucked eyebrows arched into well-simulated amazement. 'Really, Dr Westlake, I did not know that you and she were on such *intimate* terms.'

The physician endeavoured to keep a note of rebuke from creeping into his voice as he replied, 'Miss Pochin had occasion to consult me over a minor ailment. I enquired her age in the course of making my diagnosis.'

'How very odd.'

'Not in the least,' he argued, very ill-at-ease now. 'Age has a very direct bearing upon the treatment of any illness.'

She yawned behind her hand and began rearranging the folds of her sprigged muslin skirts, running her fingernail abstractedly down the creases. Without raising her head to look at him, she said 'I shall expect you at ten o'clock on Wednesday morning, sir.'

'When I shall be at your service, Miss Darker.'

She gave him her cat-smile and stared speculatively at his retreating back.

4

William's Ship Comes In

'Looks like a go-er to me.' The head groom's brief comment was torn from him in an unusual burst of spontaneity as Richard Darker led the chestnut stallion into the stables. He slid an appreciative and well-practised hand down the long length of the animal's glossy back, whistling softly between his teeth as he did so. 'A *real* go-er. 'E's not fer ridin' to 'ounds, this 'un, sir? Leastways, I 'ope 'e's not.'

'Ain't he, though?' Richard's smile, with its sly hint of mischief, confirmed Tom Gander's worst fears. 'He is my wedding-gift to the bride, Tom. D'ye think she'll take to him?'

Tom made a sound half-way between astonishment and disgust. 'She doan know good 'orseflesh if she takes *agin* 'im.' He added with terse disapproval, 'Too good for a female, 'e is. You oughter race 'im at Newmarket, sir, again the Dook o' Cumberland's Prince've 'Anover. Give 'im a race, this 'un would.'

Richard's broad, ruddy countenance cracked into mirth. 'Never were a lady's man, were ye, Tom?'

Tom was bent almost double as he inspected the stallion's fetlocks. The question drew forth a firmly dogmatic response which was slightly muffled by his exertions. 'Brings naught but a mort o' trouble, does wimmin.'

'How would ye know, ye old ruffian? Ye've never been within a mile of one so far as I know.'

'Not since I were weaned,' agreed Tom with a marked air of satisfaction. He straightened, grunting his approval of the new arrival, and clashed head-on with the hard, blue-grey stare of his master's younger brother. 'Doan show much tact, sir, if you doan mind my sayin' so. You givin' the new missis a 'orse, I mean, seein' as what 'appened last time.'

A flicker of annoyance, like the flash of summer lightning, passed across the face confronting Tom's, and the slack, indolent mouth drooped. Tom was not in the least put out by the hoisting of these flags of warning. Ten years ago a swiping backhander would have cured Master Dick of the sulks. It was necessary, now that he had grown to manhood, to use more subtle means to restore good humour.

'You knows I speaks my mind, sir, and that 'tis your good reppytation I 'as regard to.'

The placatory words had their desired effect. Richard's eyes lost their cold, accusing stare, and his mouth stretched into a smile. 'Lightning never strikes in the same place twice, Tom. There's a deal of truth in that saying.'

Tom scratched his beak of a nose. The look in his sloe-dark eyes was unforgiving. ''Tain't allus true, that old sayin', sir. Th'old elm down at Ditchley's Bottom, now. 'Er's bin struck twice. Doan show much tact,' he repeated sternly, obviously well pleased with his neat turn of phrase, 'but then, you never did.'

The undoubted veracity of this statement set them both off, and they fell into laughter, as was so often the case with these two who had long nursed a deep-rooted affection for each other. Richard was the first to recover. 'Have the chestnut saddled up by eleven tomorrow morning, Tom. I shall ride him up to Sir John Lambton's place and see what he's made of.'

'When you see what 'e's made of,' predicted Tom with airy assurance, 'you'll not want to part wi' 'im. Not to a female, anyway.'

As he made his way back to the house, hands thrust deep into his breeches pockets, Richard pondered Tom's words. What had prompted him to buy Clarissa Branson a stallion, when the memory was still fresh in everyone's minds of that other stallion he had purchased to present to his brother's first wife? A spirited beast, it had thrown her and her unborn child into eternity. The silent question remained unanswered.

Richard Darker, being of a carefree disposition, had little or no insight into the workings of his own mind. Most of his actions were performed on the spur of the moment, and if he gave to others pain, instead of the pleasure he had honestly intended, there was always someone to whom the blame could be attached. 'When your finger is in the pie, Dick,' his eldest brother had once told him, 'it always spoils.' He knew it, and yet could not seem to put a curb on his impetuosity. What more natural, he reasoned, as he sprang up the steps and entered the house, than that he should wish to present his brother's bride with a magnificent horse costing all of two hundred guineas? She would take it as a great compliment, and it would get their relationship off to a good start. Resolutely, Richard put the memory of that other woman to the back of his mind, refusing to acknowledge that his relationship with his brother's first wife had got off to so good a start that it had far exceeded the bounds of propriety.

Cornelius Darker met his brother in the hall, waving a piece of paper. 'Oh, there you are, Richard. Have you seen William?' The speaker ran a slim, nervous hand through his thatch of curling blond hair.

Richard grinned, amused as always by Cornelius's grim earnestness. 'He is down in the fallow field, trying out the new plough.'

'Oh, yes, I had forgotten.' Cornelius tugged at the handkerchief tucked into his waistband and having extracted it with some difficulty, transferred it to his moist brow. 'I have just received word from

Captain Gomez that the *Arethusa* has docked at London Bridge. We've another parcel of blacks to dispose of.'

Richard's eyebrows lifted. 'So soon? She was not expected until the end of next month.'

Cornelius stowed away the handkerchief and began toying with a gold-mounted quizzing-glass which hung from a chain about his neck. 'I know,' he agreed worriedly, 'but Captain Gomez says the winds were fair all the way from the Windward Islands.' Briefly, he consulted the letter. 'He says he has never known such a smooth passage. Only four of the slaves died.'

Cornelius's pale blue eyes searched his brother's face as though he expected a solution to this unexpected turn of events to be plainly depicted on the well-known lineaments. 'William is getting married one week from today,' he pointed out superfluously, 'which means that he will be unable to go to London until after his wedding-tour.'

'And even then he will be too much occupied to think of a few blacks.'

'Oh, please, Richard, do not jest.' Cornelius raised a deprecating hand.

'The matter is something serious. We simply cannot leave two hundred slaves on board the *Arethusa* until William can find time to go up to London.'

Richard placed both hands on his brother's shoulders and engaged his worried glance. 'My dear brother, the business is soon resolved. The tour will have to be put off for a while, and after the wedding William must take Clarissa to London. While he deals with the slaves, I have no doubt that Clarissa will pass the time pleasantly enough by visiting the gardens at Ranelagh and Vauxhall, and buying herself fine silks from the shops in Ludgate Hill. Once she gets that rather large nose of hers buried in Mantua silks and Geneva velvets she will forget all about her country-house visits. I daresay William, for his part, will be mighty relieved to have an excuse not to visit his wife's dull relations in Sussex.'

Cornelius's pursed lips emitted a thin whistle of relief. 'Do you really think so?'

'I do not doubt it for an instant. Unless of course...' Here Richard paused for a moment, assumed an air of artful innocence which did not deceive his brother for a moment, and concluded '...you take the notion to go to London yourself.'

The suggestion was not kindly received. 'Oh, no! No! I could not possibly do that. The infernal creatures smell so, and I should have to go on board to sort things out with Captain Gomez. That time last year when you and William both had the smallpox...d'ye remember? William press-ganged me into dealing with the unloading of the *Balfour Castle* when she came in.'

The memories evoked by these words were so painful to Cornelius that small beads of perspiration broke out on his brow. 'I cannot for the life of me think why, but Captain Gomez has a very disturbing effect upon me. Fellow seemed to think it necessary to expose me to the most harrowing sights imaginable. Slaves with sores, demented females shrieking abuse in their heathen tongues, and such like.' He shuddered delicately. 'It was damned unpleasant, *and* he took me below to see one of the black wenches who was giving birth. Made some tasteless remark about two for the price of one. I confess I could not look. I turned my head away, and the deuced impudent rascal actually laughed, as if he was enjoying himself at my expense!'

He was, brother, he was, Richard said

to himself, and marvelled that Cornelius had not yet come to realise that his affected airs made him the butt of any low fellow who cared to bandy words with him. Cornelius would be happier residing in London, thought Richard, where his little peculiarities would be viewed with a more indulgent eye than they were here in Piddingfold. It was noticeable, however, that some of those who mocked his brother were glad enough to purchase the smuggled goods which mysteriously turned up from time to time, and were dispensed by Cornelius with all the benevolence of the squire's lady handing out bowls of charity soup. The significant difference was, of course, that the youngest Mr Darker's services were requited with gleaming coin of the realm, while the squire's lady must rest content with a deferential bow and an uncertain smile. Cornelius had proved himself to be remarkably adept over the illegal traffic of dutiable goods. He owned a small sailing dinghy which plied regularly between Newporth and Dieppe, right under the noses of the revenue men, bearing carefully concealed cargoes of brandy, Geneva, tobacco, tea and sugar.

Richard was reminded to issue a warning.

He smiled easily at his brother as the latter fussily smoothed the skirts of his plum-coloured frock-coat, and gave a twitch to the falls of lace at his wrists. 'Do not mention your nefarious dealings with our friends in France to the new bride. She may hold the same absurdly high-handed ideas as her father on that score. Sir Charles must be the only land-owner in these parts who holds smugglers in poor esteem.'

Cornelius looked thoroughly taken aback. 'D'ye think she would tell tales on me? Her own brother-in-law?'

Richard shrugged. 'Who can say for sure? Miss Clarissa Branson is an unknown quantity as yet. We've still to get to know her.'

An expression of undisguised chagrin greeted these worrying observations. ''Pox on it then. I had saved her a twenty-pound bag of Hyson's tea.' He volunteered hopefully, 'I could say that I paid duty on it.'

Richard threw back his head and gave his laughter full rein. 'You could,' he agreed between outbreaks of mirth. 'She might even believe you.'

Cornelius's forehead creased into lines of anxiety. 'Fan me, ye winds, but I do think it mighty uncivil of William to choose a bride whose father is a Justice of the Peace and a Member of Parliament to boot.'

This sent Richard off into more noisy and explosive bursts of sound. Dr Westlake, descending the stairs at this precise moment, thought, not for the first time, what a remarkably vociferous family he had secured as his patients. There was nothing calm or dignified about the Darkers.

Catching sight of the physician, Cornelius, who hated all things vaguely appertaining to medicine, bade the newcomer a hasty 'Good morning, sir,' and was gone with cowardly speed. Richard stood his ground, stared at the physician with coolly raised eyebrows, and asked after the health of his sister.

Dr Westlake quickly assumed his mask of authoritarian professionalism, which he had discovered was his only defence against the gentry's general air of condescending insolence, and pronounced Miss Darker to be pretty fair, save for a certain agitation of the humours which would shortly pass under his ministrations.

'Jumpy, is she?' observed Richard easily, and saw the physician blink with surprise. 'That will pass when the wedding is over.

She was not very partial to my brother's first wife, and I daresay it will be the same with the second. Since our mother died the competition of another female in the house has invariably proved too much for her constitution. If my father were alive he'd beat the foolishness out of her.'

'I...that is to say, I...'

'Yes?' Richard's unrelenting eyes bored into the physician's face in a manner which the other found extremely disconcerting. Now that he had embarked upon a statement, however, Dr Westlake felt impelled to go on, if only to dislodge the penetrating regard which held him prisoner.

'Well, sir...I thought I might venture to suggest to Mr Darker that Miss Darker should shortly...er, that is to say, marry...for the good of her health.'

The troublesome, unfriendly eyes became even more interested, and their victim actually felt himself blushing under their merciless and protracted scrutiny. Richard cocked his head to one side in quizzical appraisal. 'Been at you, has she?'

Dr Westlake was covered in confusion. 'No, I...no...most assuredly *not!* I would not presume...' His voice tailed off as he experienced a warm feeling spreading under his neckband. He lapsed into wretched, impotent silence.

Richard's grin was sardonic. 'I am well aware, sir, that you would not presume, but Miss Darker is not so delicate in her manners. She would *presume.*'

A mocking imitation of his own rather clipped style of speech put the physician at an even greater disadvantage. He made a futile attempt to regain the initiative. 'I hardly think, sir...'

Rudely, Richard interrupted him. 'If you feel uneasy with my sister, man, why do you not enlist the services of the worthy Miss Pochin to satisfy the demands of propriety?'

Stiffly came the reply. 'Miss Darker prefers that I see her alone.'

At this Richard allowed his contempt to show. 'What sort of milk-sop fellow are ye, sir? Tell her you will not see her alone. If you cannot handle a sixteen-year-old girl with the green-sickness, perhaps it is time my brother found us another saw-bones.'

The physician was now mashed to a proper and meek humility. He said, 'Sir, by your leave, I will in future insist that Miss Pochin remains in attendance during my consultations with Miss Darker. Unfortunately, Miss Darker is inclined to be a trifle importunate...I...'

Richard, impatient to end the distasteful interview, at last took pity on his social inferior and promised grimly, 'I shall speak to my sister. You will have no more trouble in that quarter.'

'I am obliged to you, sir.' Dr Westlake bowed and managed a dignified exit, but as he climbed into his phaeton a slow-burning, murderous rage took possession of him and began to smoulder in his breast. It was a rage directed solely at his own undoubted inferiority.

5

Patience Pochin Takes Stock

Patience Pochin watched the departure of the physician's phaeton with a lingering sigh of regret. The number of eligible gentlemen who encroached upon the periphery of her tightly circumscribed world was lamentably few, and it was all the more vexing, therefore, to be continually thwarted in her efforts to converse with one of these rare creatures by the wicked machinations of that spiteful creature Sophie.

With a low moan of sheer frustration Patience removed her wide-brimmed grey felt bonnet, daringly trimmed with pink ribbon, and shrugged off her well-worn merino cloak. Miss Sophie Darker, palpitating with awareness of the physician's imminent arrival, had cunningly devised a very particular errand upon which to send her cousin, that is to say the purchase of a pot of red lip-salve and a phial of bella-donna, her intense female vanity convincing her that these dangerous cosmetics would enhance her small pretensions to beauty.

Seating herself at her small boudoir-table, Patience studied her image in the oval mirror which had to be wedged with a wad of paper to keep it at the correct angle. 'Homespun,' she said aloud. 'Your features, Miss Patience, are decidedly homespun and devoid of vitality.' She was less than just, and gave herself no marks for a flawlessly smooth complexion, a high forehead, betokening a degree of intellect far in excess of those whom she considered her social superiors, and wide-set, thoughtful greenish-grey eyes which surveyed the world about her with uncomfortable directness. Her nose and mouth, it is true, were somewhat insignificant, being neither classical nor boldly plebian in appearance. Indeed, the latter, forced by her circumstances to stay firmly closed upon any trivial remark she might be indiscreet enough to utter in the presence of her wealthy cousins, seemed to the casual observer to be a convenience she could well have done without, had it not been essential for the purpose of conveying food to her stomach.

Patience's lint-pale hair was plaited to within an inch of its life. No fashionable frizzlation for her, or those long corkscrew curls into which the gentlemen seemed to find it well-nigh imperative to poke their fingers. In her maiden state she alone could gaze upon its unbound luxuriance in the privacy of her bedchamber, and arrange the curling tendrils upon her forehead before she blew out the candle.

She was soon done with the contemplation of her under-rated countenance, but she had not failed to notice the faint red mark on the side of her neck which betokened things not willingly recalled. The mark was a part of her other life, the secret portion of her existence which she refused openly to acknowledge. It was as if she had her being upon two separate levels. The first offered her reality, an environment peopled with familiar faces and loud, commanding voices; the second, a dim world, a realm of near-fantasy, inhabited by only one person other than herself. Lately she had suspected that this denizen of her nether-world was not being entirely frank with her. She had listened to half-truths, silken reassurances and promises which she had begun to suspect were false, with a growing faintness of heart and a sickening sense of having lost the winning throw in a monstrous gamble. She must now endeavour to recoup her losses by means of a venture less ambitious.

The strategy of this new venture having been determined upon, she could not but regard it as exceeding ill-luck that she had not encountered Dr Westlake when she returned to the house. She judged that she must have entered the house and begun her ascent of the back-stairs at the precise moment that the physician was in the process of descending by the hall staircase.

The total unfairness of life was suddenly borne in upon Patience, and the strangled feeling in her throat which heralded the onset of tears, combined with the creeping suspicion that her dream-world was about to collapse about her ears, took her by surprise. She gulped away the momentary weakness and resolutely directed her thoughts towards more practical matters. Unlocking her *bureau-champêtre,* which she had previously extracted from beneath her narrow bed—its regular habitat having regard to Sophie's prying ways—she examined its contents and found herself to be the possessor of several letters from her father, post prepaid, a garnet brooch and the sum of eight guineas, the latter secured in a draw-string chamois leather bag.

She did some rapid sums in her head and came to the conclusion that she could ill afford a new gown, even for so auspicious occasion as a wedding. On the other hand, this argument could be counter-balanced by an even stronger one to the effect that expenditure on material for a new gown might pay out handsome dividends in the long run. Many and varied were the weapons which could be employed to engage the attentions of a prospective suitor. At the age of twenty-five Patience had discovered that desperation was beginning to insinuate its way into her brain like some slow-killing disease.

She thought of her father, a struggling lawyer's clerk in the firm of Messrs Hackett and Booth of Church Lane, Hounslow, of her mother, worn out with her struggle merely to survive, of her seven younger sisters, all of whom still existed on their father's patrimony. How elated they would be if she could make a good match. It would give her unmarried sisters the encouragement they so badly needed.

Boldly, Patience selected two guineas from her dwindling savings, unable to restrain a feeling of warmth at her own extravagance and undoubted vanity. After locking the bureau and replacing it under the bed, she picked up the pot of lip-salve and the phial of bella-donna, and hurried along to her charge's room.

Sophie looked like the cat who had got at the cream. Her former listlessness in the presence of the physician had miraculously dissolved, and she was trying the effect of a length of peacock-blue silk which she had draped over her shoulder, twisting from side to side before the long cheval-glass in order to admire her reflection.

'Do you think the colour suits me, Patience? Cornelius gave it to me.'

Patience suppressed a twinge of pure envy, brought on by the rapid calculation that the expensive length of material must be worth at least fifteen shillings a yard. She said reprovingly, 'Why do you solicit my opinion, Sophie, when you have already made up your mind that the colour will look extremely well on you?'

Sophie stared back at her cousin truculently. 'You should be flattered, Patience, that I place any value at all upon your opinion. The daughter of a lawyer's clerk can hardly presume to set herself up as an authority upon the *beau monde.*'

Patience was used to such cutting remarks issuing from the lips of her cousin. After three years they no longer had the power to wound deeply. Had it not been for the proximity of Dr Westlake she might now have considered leaving Frinton Park and seeking a post as a governess somewhere, but there was much to be hoped for in that quarter, and she intended to wait upon that hope until it should sweetly bloom or wither in the bud. If to remain with her rich cousins meant that she must develop a hard outer shell, that shell should be grown to the thickness of plate armour to protect her against the slights so carelessly meted out to one who had not the advantage of a fortune at her disposal.

With a bright, unmeaning smile she turned the conversation. 'Did Dr Westlake prescribe anything for your pain?'

'Some horrid-tasting brew,' Sophie replied off-handedly. 'You can go down to the apothecary to get it made up after supper.'

'Cannot Annie do that?' inquired Patience, with a mildness of demeanour belied by her inward thoughts, and knowing before she asked what the answer would be.

'Annie is my *personal* maid. I want her to curl my hair. Sir John and Lady Lambton are coming over for cards.'

Patience did not essay any further argument upon the subject of the prescription. It had suddenly occurred to her that the apothecary's shop was situated within a mere stone's throw of Dr Westlake's house, and that she just might chance to encounter that gentleman as he emerged for his evening stroll, complete with malacca cane and fashionable tricorne hat. She started violently as Sophie deposited the length of silk on the bed and remarked with sly innuendo, 'If you should chance to meet Dr Westlake, take care that he does not delay you with idle conversation.'

Patience went very red, and said with a mixture of indignation and anger, 'I am not in the habit of gossiping in the street with casual acquaintances.'

Sophie shrieked with laughter, a sound which grated quite horribly on her cousin's nerves. 'Mere acquaintances, indeed! I am not so easily deceived as you may think.'

'And what, pray, do you mean by that, Miss?' Quite forgetting, it seemed, her inferior position, Patience began to show outward manifestations of the rage bottled up inside her, and, casting caution to the winds, advanced upon the astonished Sophie in a manner frankly menacing.

Sophie, quickly reasoning that cousin Patience was hardly likely to assault her physically, nevertheless retreated a step or two before saying coldly, 'I do not believe that I am required to explain to *you* every remark which slips from my tongue. Your attitude and tone offend me. If you value your place here, you will never speak to me in that way again.'

But her adversary was not to be put off. Wrath made her bold. 'I do not value my *place* so highly,' said she, 'that I will suffer the insolence of a spoiled brat who has quite forgot her manners.'

Sophie's pale eyes bulged, but such was Patience's usefulness to her in a hundred ways that she bit back the retort which sprang to her lips, and which would have instantly despatched her cousin to pack her bags, and contented herself with, 'I meant only that you have often cast sheep's eyes at Dr Westlake. Now that you cannot deny.'

'But I do deny it, most vehemently,' returned Patience, 'and you will oblige me, Sophie, by never mentioning the subject again.'

The other girl shrugged and turned away, and flinging herself down on the bed, began idly to pick at the embroidered motifs on the coverlet. Her eyes remained lowered as she said, 'You had better not entertain any hopes in that direction. Dr Westlake is a man of ambition. You would not do for him at all.'

For the second time that day Patience

came dangerously close to tears. Before she could humiliate herself further she turned her back on the mischievous girl, and murmuring that she must change for supper, left the room. She had her revenge the next day when a furious Sophie was told unequivocally by her brother Richard that in future she was on no account to see Dr Westlake without the chaperonage of her cousin.

6

Clarissa Speaks Her Mind

'I think you are the most fortunate creature alive to be marrying Mr Darker.'

Ann Branson, fifteen years old, and deeply affected by her perusal of Mr Samuel Richardson's *Pamela,* in which the course of true love was so harrowingly portrayed, carefully folded her eldest sister's fur-trimmed pelisse and placed it in the smart new leather travelling valise, with its gleaming brass studs and locks.

Clarissa, mounted upon a low occasional table, like a statue symbolising virtue, revolved slowly at the dressmaker's behest, in order that the hem of her bridal gown might be adjusted to the correct length. Made of white figured satin, with tucked bodice and little puffed sleeves, it gave to her too-thin, girlish figure the womanly curves which it did not in reality possess. Falls of lace at wrists and neck added that all-important air of fragility so necessary to a bride, a look of porcelain delicacy which caused women to weep as they dimly recalled their own lost innocence, and men to lust, remembering their filching of that perishable commodity.

Her youngest sister's enthusiasm made Clarissa smile. 'Your opinion, my dearest Ann,' she observed, 'is based solely upon the fact that Mr Darker flatters you outrageously, chucks you under the chin and calls you "Miss Bright-Eyes".'

Ann giggled as she ran her capable little hands over the smooth green velvet of the pelisse. 'He says that I am sure to make the very best match in the county when I come out.'

'Then does he not think that *I* am making the best match in the county?'

inquired her sister with a sidelong, mischievous glance which put Mrs Bridges, the dressmaker, in imminent danger of swallowing a mouthful of pins.

Georgiana, the plainest of the three girls, and therefore she who was least opinionated, closed the lid of one of Clarissa's bonnet boxes, having deposited therein an exquisite creation of satin and feathers, and remarked with her usual air of quiet charm, 'I think, Clarissa, that Mr Darker is an extremely kind gentleman. At least, he has always appeared so to me.'

Kindness was not a characteristic which Clarissa would have attributed to her future husband, but she did not say so. To put her feelings about him into words would have made her feel foolish. How was it possible to express her sense of a lurking presence hidden behind that genial, easy-going façade, and rather heavily bucolic features, give it form or substance, adequately describe it?

Her thoughts turned to Frances Lacey, that other woman in William Darker's life, whose painted images, at least three or four of them, stared down at her from the walls of Frinton Park, so soon to be her new home. There was nothing hostile or sinister about the dark-eyed, serious regard of the woman who had preceded her, and yet the very indifference, the haughty acceptance of fate which seemed to be denoted by the facial expression, gave one the impression that Frances had turned inwards upon herself and secured the locks upon secrets which she would never reveal to the world.

Clarissa had not known the living Frances well. Polite greetings and formal conversations had equalled the sum of their intercourse. Perhaps that was why she felt a compulsion to study the portrait, to force an inner, more intimate communion between herself and the dead woman which had never existed in life. The exercise had been a fruitless one. The images, while hinting at mystery, were no more willing to reveal the true nature of that mystery than had been the living flesh. Had it even been out of character, Clarissa wondered, for Frances, six months gone with child, to go galloping off on that spirited stallion with such scant regard for her own safety and that of her unborn child? The reckless action did not fit in with the quietly confident mien she presented to the world.

Ann, who was dealing now with the weird intricacies of feminine under-garments, startled Clarissa out of her reverie by announcing that Mr Darker had promised her the gift of a black boy the very next time one of his slave-ships docked. The imparting of this intelligence deepened the frown on Clarissa's forehead, a thin line of anxiety which had been imprinted there ever since her mind had become occupied with her predecessor.

The dressmaker having signified that the hem of her gown was satisfactorily pinned, Clarissa jumped down from the table and extended her arms above her head while the woman divested her of her pristine finery. 'It was quite wrong of Mr Darker to suggest such a thing,' she told Ann, 'without first consulting Papa upon the matter. Had he done so, I am quite sure that Papa, knowing my views upon the subject of the slave-trade, with its bartering of human flesh, would have refused the offer.'

Not a whit put off by her youngest sister's downcast looks, Clarissa continued to enlarge upon the miseries endured by the miserable wretches who were made to submit to the long voyage from the West

Indian islands, chained to hard wooden bunks below decks, and in many cases lying in their own ordure and vomit. There were, she believed, instances of women giving birth in these filthy conditions, and it was undoubtedly true that many did not survive the voyages. Young black girls often fell victim to the vile lust of common sailors.

This unladylike recital had a wonderfully sobering effect upon her sisters and left Mrs Bridges positively aghast. The latter, a rosy-cheeked, rigidly respectable countrywoman, whose family had served the Bransons for many years, made bold to ask, rather breathlessly, exactly how Miss Branson could have come by such horrid information.

Miss Branson, having bent upon the dressmaker a look of infinite severity, begged leave to inform her, with uncharacteristic brusqueness, that anyone who cared to might read Mr Granville Sharp's articles in *The London Advertiser,* and thus learn the unpalatable truth for themselves. 'Mr Granville Sharp,' she went on to instruct in her 'governessy' voice—so dubbed by the irrepressible Ann—'has spoken out against this abominable traffic, but I fear that he has a great many people to convince of its shamefulness, poor gentleman, before he can accomplish anything worthwhile.'

Mrs Bridges tut-tutted vaguely and took refuge in her work on the bridal gown. Georgiana said anxiously, 'I trust that you will not make your views known to Mr Darker, Clarry. I am informed that he owns two slave-ships and employs three or four slaves for his own field work. It would be most unfortunate if you were to begin married life together upon a quarrel.'

Clarissa bit her lip. 'Have no fear on that score, Georgiana. The spirit is willing, but the courage is lacking.'

Ann, whose brown eyes still held remnants of the shock occasioned by Clarry's forthright views, asked curiously, 'What shall you do about the little black boy up at Frinton Park? Shall you try to set him free?'

Clarissa shrugged her thin shoulders and stepped into her day-gown, helpfully held out to her by Georgiana. 'Where would he go, poor little thing? At least he is well cared for now that the damage has been done, and his duties are not arduous.'

'I wonder what they will do with him when he is grown up?' Georgiana asked thoughtfully. 'He will hardly be suited to work in the fields.'

Clarissa's eyes gleamed with the light of battle. 'Perhaps by then the law will have been changed, and he will be free to go where he will,' she said.

The door of the morning-room opened and the girls' mother came in, a short, plump personage, over-burdened with orange-tawny satin and lace flounces. Her ample bosom, laced into monumental immobility, turned the top half of her into the semblance of a ship's figurehead, a simile not inapt, for Lady Branson breasted her way through life with much the same careless disregard for her paintwork. Rouge and lip-salve were the hallmarks of her grim determination to cling tenaciously to the bloom of youth for as long as art and nature permitted.

Her mouse-brown hair, piled on top of her head, had been subjected to the complicated operation of frizzlation three months ago and was now in urgent need of further attentions from the hairdresser. She intended to have her head re-done for her daughter's wedding, but rather balked at the long and uncomfortable processes of twisting, burning and greasing which it involved. The odour of rancid grease which she now carried about with her, like an unwelcome second presence, was becoming a trifle persistent in its clinging qualities—one had only to walk into a room to know that Lady Branson had but recently left it—and the business could not long be delayed.

Elizabeth Branson had once been as pleasing to look upon as her eldest daughter, but having unwisely applied the first layer of white lead paste to a blooming fourteen-year-old cheek some thirty years previously, and continued the process ever since, this was, inevitably, no longer the case. She had sacrificed much on the altar of beauty, but the gods no longer accepted her offerings. She was a harmless woman, imbued with very little malice, whose sole burning desire was to see her daughters well settled in life and 'looked up to' in the county. Her time and not inconsiderable energies were dissipated in the attainment of these ends, which she saw as the biggest single challenge of her existence. The challenge met and conquered, Lady Branson would have very little left to live for. Her beaming smile was all-embracing as her daughters curtsied and Mrs Bridges lifted her well-rounded posterior a couple of inches from the chair and said, 'Good morning, m'lady.'

Lady Branson's blue eyes gave forth an embarrassingly sentimental glow as she examined the bridal gown and smoothed its rich surface with tender fingers. 'This will be the wedding of the year in the county, my dears,' she exulted.

Turning to Clarissa, who, with the aid of a hand-mirror, was carefully examining her face for any sinister indications of ageing, or perhaps the sneaking up of a blemish or two to spoil her wedding-day face, she said with waggish enthusiasm, 'My dear, your Papa has just this moment returned from Lewes. Mr Darker was there too, having had business to transact at the bank, and chancing to meet your Papa at the "White Hart", informed him that your wedding-tour is to commence in London! Think of it, Clarissa, London at the commencement of the *season!*' She added excitedly, 'Should you be so fortunate as to see any of the Royal Family, be sure to take particular notice of their looks, especially with regard to the King's aunts and sisters, and let us know if they are like their portraits. Lady Lambton has a copy of Mr Zoffany's portrait of Queen Charlotte in which the eyes appear to be blue, but I have always supposed them to be more green than blue.'

Lady Branson had gone quite pink with the pleasure of it all. Not so Clarissa, who was staring at her mother with blank disappointment written plainly on her face. 'But, Mama, I was so looking forward to going to Aunt Clara's for the spring ball, and of visiting our Brookwood cousins at Findon.' Tears sprang to her eyes. 'I hate London in the season!'

Her mother looked distressed. 'But, my dearest child, you *must* go to London. One of Mr Darker's ships is newly docked, and is to be unloaded and the cargo disposed of.'

'Cargo!' exclaimed Clarissa, in so loud a voice that her mother jumped. 'You are speaking of human beings, Mama! The cargo to which you refer consists of men, women and little children, all torn from their native lands to be sold into slavery.'

'Oh, oh, heavens!' Lady Branson looked at Ann and Georgiana in turn. 'Your sister is distraught, my dears. It is very natural on the day before her wedding. I remember how very nervous I was, only in my case I could scarcely speak at all.' Lady Branson looked as though she wished very much that Clarissa had been similarly affected. She concluded practically, 'Ann, my dear child, please to ask Cook if she can spare Heppy to run down to the village and ask the apothecary for a soothing draught. A small dose will calm your sister's nerves and ensure that she has a good night's sleep.'

'Mama!' wailed Clarissa. 'You do not *understand!*'

'I assure you that I do, my dearest child. I understand perfectly,' countered her mother, endeavouring to appear calm, 'and I am sure you will feel quite restored when you have taken a dose. Oh!' She brightened, struck by a sudden thought. 'I quite forgot to tell you that Mr Richard Darker has bought a horse for you to ride to hounds.'

'He bought Frances Lacey a horse,' said Ann before she could stop herself.

'The brute which threw her,' put in Clarissa swiftly.

'Because she was foolish enough to ride when she was six months gone with child,' said their mother sharply. 'She was a proud, wilful woman.'

Clarissa stared at her mother in surprise. 'She was a courteous, quiet sort of person, Mama.'

Lady Branson declined to hear this contrary opinion. She knew what she knew. 'Ann,' she commanded briskly, 'go this instant and speak to Cook. There is just time before Mr Sheldon comes to give you your music lesson.'

7

Clarissa And William Are Married

At five o'clock on the morning of his wedding day, William Darker stood with his dog on the top of Piddingfold Down and surveyed his domain. As far as his eyes could see the land was his, a giant's patchwork quilt, made up of crops and rolling pastures which undulated for over two miles towards the valley bottom. Away to his left he could see the young corn springing greenly from the ploughed furrows of the richly-manured earth, so tender as yet that his fancy likened it to a gauze veil flung over the body of a young West Indian woman. What a sight it would be just before cutting time, when the tall corn bent before the south-west wind and flowed onwards towards the horizon like a swirling yellow sea.

William's intent and loving gaze travelled westwards, down into Ditchley Bottom and up again to the other side, the very summit of the hill, crowned by the house his grandfather had built in 1727 out of the proceeds of the slave trade. A good, solid edifice it was too, rooted deep in the Sussex soil, and with few ornamental fripperies to spoil its uncluttered lines. Straight out of Sir John Vanbrugh's pattern book was Frinton Park, copied by local craftsmen with such faithful adherence to detail that the master himself would not have been ashamed to put his mark upon it.

From where William stood, looking down from his lofty eminence, not much of the house was visible, a hint of rose-red brick glimpsed through the thick fringe of elms which bordered the lawns, one or two square chimney-stacks, from which the smoke was already beginning to rise in thin blue curls, the nesting-holes of a ruined medieval dove-cot, sole remaining relic of the previous house which had stood on that same site since the thirteenth century. The mausoleum, built on the lines of the much admired Temple of Diana at Blenheim Palace, with pedimented roof and Doric columns, was completely hidden from view by the trees. Behind the house the land gradually dropped away again, down to the inlet and Witham Cove where Cornelius kept his boat. On a clear day you could just catch sight of the silver sparkle of the sea from where he was standing now.

A warm glow of affection pervaded William's whole being as he shaded his eyes with his hand and stared across the valley at his home. He was primitive man, basking in the knowledge that his cave offered him security from the hazards of predators, the freezing winter winds and the unknown world beyond the confines of his territory. All about him were scattered the ewes, with the new season's crop of lambs hanging to their teats and bleating more strongly with the passing of each day. It had been a good year, with one hundred and eighty lambs dropped and only three not managing to survive a treacherously frosty spring.

The old bell-wether clanked noisily

towards William to chew the cud within a yard from where he stood. He bent down and dug his fingers into the thick, springy growth of wool which covered her broad back. Head down, she moved slowly away from him; he allowed her back to run under his hand, giving a final, playful tweak to her tail as she went beyond his reach. It was marvellous what satisfaction a man's sense of touch could give him. Wood, wool, corn husks, a horse's smooth flank, they all had their own special feel, a grand feel. He liked the feel of wool best of all. The mere thought of wool was enough to make his mouth water, as though he were smelling the appetising aroma of food.

The chiming of the church clock brought William to his senses and to the realisation that it lacked but five hours to the time appointed for his wedding. There was a great deal of work to be done before he could don his wedding-clothes and set off for the church. All at once, up there on the hill, with the silent spaniel crouching at his feet, he began to experience a nameless, inward dread, an odd sense of vulnerability which caused him to sway very slightly on his feet. There is nothing more alarming to a man than the moment when the stability of his world appears to be in question. The feeling passed swiftly enough, to be followed by one of slight panic. He was thirty years old, an age when a man begins to think of his own mortality, complete and final if he does not have a son to follow in his wake. Sons, not one, but many, to revive and support him in his declining years.

Frances might have given him a son. The memory of his first wife flared into life, inevitably bound up with his need for a male heir to inherit his property. What had happened before must not be allowed to happen again. Richard's gift of a stallion to Clarissa had been like an iron gauntlet flung in his face. He had refused to take up the challenge, because to do so would have shown a weakness and uncertainty which his brother would have pounced upon and exploited to the full.

As he descended the hill, walking with measured stride, the dog obediently at heel, William asked himself why he had not simply turned his brother out of doors with a few guineas and a letter of introduction to Colonel Baxter of the 10th Hussars. The answer to that, he decided, was because he was too stiff-necked to admit defeat at the hands of a meddling ne'er-do-well like Dick, who had never ceased to resent the fact that Frinton Park and all its vast acreage would never be his...unless, and here William's fists balled together with impotent fury at the prospect of dying childless and leaving his patrimony to one who would dissipate it in the pursuance of his favourite pastimes, namely, gaming and women.

Into the teeth of the wind William flung his veto. 'It shall not happen again!' The wind whispered back, calling him a name which he refused to acknowledge.

The wedding-party drove home at an enforced leisurely pace from the parish church, hemmed in by a laughing, shouting crowd of boisterous villagers, who contested every inch of the way and did their level best to impede the progress of the bride and groom, making the former blush with their frank and unsolicited advice to her husband.

At frequent intervals unconcerted blasts from trumpet, bugle and horn rent the air, interspersed with the harsh rattle of bird-scarers, wielded by little boys who exerted considerably more energy than they displayed when employing these instruments for their more legitimate purposes. Babies in arms added their strident howls to the general hideous cacophony of sound, and it seemed to Clarissa that the whole world had turned out to greet her on her wedding day.

At the gates of Frinton Park willing hands unharnessed the horses, and a dozen or so eager lads placed themselves between the shafts of the carriage to manhandle it for the remaining half-mile of gravelled driveway leading to the main door. The slight delay occasioned by the unhitching of the horses had caused a pile-up of six or seven vehicles behind the bridal carriage, the male occupants of which hooted and whistled, brandished their whips, and generally behaved like small boys let out of school. Good-humoured badinage was exchanged, and there began a frantic jostling for places, as if it were of the utmost importance to arrive as soon as possible after the bride and 'groom.

At this, the ladies' high-pitched voices could be heard raised in airy protest, and little screams of dismay piped forth as gowns and hair-styles became disarranged. Failing to bring order among their playful menfolk, the ladies at last gave up their efforts to restore order, and alighting from the carriages, walked up to the house in colourful and dignified procession across the lawn. This gave the gentlemen *carte-blanche* to pursue their childish games, with the result that the ensuing mad scramble up the drive resulted in three broken heads and a profusion of swelling bruises.

Lady Branson, walking beside her sister-in-law, Charlotte, whose feather-bedecked head topped hers by at least six inches, commented sadly, 'God knows what the end of this day will bring. The gentlemen have not yet drunk half a bottle apiece!'

Three hours after the foregoing frenzied activity, the guests, feeling fairly replete—although one or two were still inclined to nibble at fruit and sweetmeats—made their way up to the first-floor saloon, transformed for the occasion into a ballroom. This was a magnificent chamber which William, shortly after his father's death, had had redesigned entirely in Adam style, right down to the beautifully-wrought gilt door knobs. The delicate-toned carpet, designed to faithfully reproduce the garlands and medallions on the stucco-work ceiling, had been made by Thomas Witty in his Axminster factory; and the chimney-piece of Sienna marble, with its Etruscan motifs, came from Thomas Carter of Piccadilly. The whole had cost William Darker ten thousand pounds.

William had furnished the saloon with pieces from the Chippendale workshop. Satinwood tables rubbed shoulders with elegantly turned chairs and sofas, all upholstered in blue silk brocade. The tables were adorned with Blue John stoneware from Derbyshire and Wedgwood vases, and presiding over all was a magnificent six-branched candelabra purchased from Matthew Barton, who had made a similar piece for Queen Charlotte's drawing-room at Buckingham House.

After having loudly applauded a minuet danced by the bride and 'groom, the gay company thoughtfully rested their abused and overworked stomachs and allowed the normal processes of digestion to begin before the announcement that a buffet awaited their attention in the eating-room sent them scuttling off downstairs to commit further atrocities upon their internal organs.

Miss Charlotte Branson, whose fifty-eight years sat lightly upon her, cornered

Mr Cornelius Darker in the library, where that gentleman had gone to seek asylum from importunate, 'in-the-know' persons, all begging, finger to nose, for some of his fine French brandy, and placing a conspiratorial finger to her lips enquired politely, and a thought roguishly, if he would be so good as to procure for her a length of Brussels brocade, as she had a great fancy to appear at the next assembly ball in something which would be the envy of all the other ladies.

The request, implying as it did that Miss Charlotte, the sister of a local magistrate, did not share her brother's anti-smuggling views, came as a mildly embarrassing surprise to Cornelius. He found himself at a loss for words and tried to bluster his way out of the awkward situation by attempting to convince Miss Charlotte that she had approached the wrong party. Miss Charlotte's plump red cheeks fattened into a knowing smile. She tossed her bronze curls, attached, alas, to a gauze base, and wagged her finger at Cornelius. 'Wicked boy,' she admonished. 'I know all about that little boat of yours, and I think it excessively ill-natured of you never to have asked me if I should like to buy something which came all the way from France.'

Hastily, Cornelius moved to the door of the library, which stood slightly ajar, and back-heeled it shut. Miss Charlotte's voice had a certain carrying quality which frightened the life out of him. Deciding that denials were useless in the face of such conclusive evidence that one elderly female knew exactly what she was talking about, he inquired in a subdued voice as to whether she had...er, in short, did Sir Charles...?

'Oh, my dear sir!' Miss Charlotte threw up her fat little hands is dismay at the mere suggestion. 'Your secret shall go with me to the *grave!* Do not, I beg you, think of me as a menace to your activities. Indeed, were I ten years younger I should come with you, instead of wasting my life by running about like a chicken with its head cut off visiting my relations, none of whom want to be bothered with me.'

Cornelius stared at Charlotte in frank and undisguised amazement. 'Dam'me, ma'am,' he muttered, 'but ye've given me the devil of a turn. May I make so bold as to ask how ye found me out? I'd lay a wager there's not a soul in Piddingfold who has rattled about me.'

Charlotte looked immensely pleased with herself. 'My dear young man, I do not sleep at all well, and it is often my custom to take a walk in the small hours of the morning. The last time I visited my brother Charles...in September, I believe it was...or was I with Clara then?' Her forehead puckered into a frown, a condition to which it was not at all accustomed, while Cornelius fidgeted impatiently and began to see the light of day.

'Yes, yes, it *was* September,' confirmed Miss Charlotte at last, nodding her head vigorously. 'I remember because I was due to go to Clara's afterwards, and I thought how tedious it would be to have to spend a month there with all those silly girls falling over each other to find husbands, and almost coming to blows over one particular gentleman of their acquaintance, a foppish, conceited fellow, in my opinion. He quoted Robert Herrick at me all the time, and recited depressing little poems all about dead children...'

'In September you said, ma'am?' interjected Cornelius doggedly.

'What? Oh, yes...' Miss Charlotte brought her craft reluctantly back on course. 'Well, as I said before, I was taking the air, down by the inlet, and I saw you coming from Witham Cove with two other gentlemen whom I could not possibly recognise, for they were muffled to the ears by their cloaks.'

'Forgive me, ma'am,' Cornelius said faintly, 'but how on earth did you recognise *me?*'

Her blue eyes mocked his air of bewilderment. 'By your hair, you foolish young man. It is of such a distinctive colour, and it shows up very pale, you know, on a dark night. I remember thinking at the time that it was most imprudent of you not to wear a hat.'

Cornelius inwardly confessed to feeling rather stupid and cursed himself for a dolt. A man should never allow carelessness to overcome discretion.

Miss Charlotte was regarding him with her head on one side. 'I shall never tell a living soul.'

Her earnest tone convinced him and his face split into a grin. 'Ma'am, I am deeply grateful. You shall have your length of brocade with my compliments.'

Miss Charlotte bounced forward and planted a kiss on his cheek. 'Dearest boy. If ever you want to *hide* anything, bring it over to my little cottage at Pysamber. I have a nice big cellar there.'

Cornelius shook with laughter.

Richard Darker danced with Ann Branson three times before steering her out into the garden and directing her footsteps towards the old dove-cot, almost a mile away. One or two wedding-guests, who were also taking a turn in the gardens, nodded and smiled as they passed the young couple, and speculated upon the likelihood of yet another wedding in the Darker family. The ladies, not failing to notice Miss Ann Branson's unchaperoned condition, frowned slightly, but their host's fine wines had had their effect, inducing in most of them a certain lethargy which quelled disquietude.

Richard was not quite sure why he had executed the manoeuvre of disengaging Ann from the mainstream of guests. She was much too immature for his taste and, in any case, he had an invitation to visit his mistress four hours from now, a longed-for release from the monotony of his days which would occupy his time and energies until the morning. Perhaps it was Ann's frankly adoring glances which had flattered him to the point where indulgence ended and titillation began.

As for Ann, never in the whole of her life had she felt so elated. Her heart was beating so fast that she felt sure he must notice its frantic fluttering under her pink taffeta bodice. In six months' time perhaps she too would be a bride, looking even more ravishing than Clarry in her white satin and lace, riding home from the church in a carriage and pair, with Richard sitting beside her and holding her hand.

As she walked along, Ann kept her eyes downcast while she waited for her escort to start a conversation, and was a little disappointed when he remarked that the park was looking well and the new Italian garden satisfactorily taking shape. In *Pamela,* even though the heroine had been seduced by her wicked employer, the gentleman had used such pretty speeches to trap her! Ann consoled herself with the thought that Richard was too reserved to begin flattering her straight away. Perhaps he thought she might be offended. How could she let him see that she would not, without seeming bold?

The dove-cot, in its ruined state, was open to the sky, forming a half-circle round a grassy plot which in summer boasted a thick carpet of golden buttercups. The nesting-holes in the section of wall that remained were still intact, and provided comfortable shelter for terns in the breeding-season. The birds were there now, and set up a little flutter at the human invasion.

The walk to the dove-cot had been covered by their young legs in pretty short order and still nothing really significant had been said, not unless you counted his reference to her eyes matching the colour of his horse. He had been teasing her when he said that, just as if she was a little girl. As she sat down on the crumbling stone ledge beneath the nesting-holes, Ann could feel the prick of tears behind her eyelids. Suddenly, as she gazed miserably into her lap, a hard brown hand covered hers and a cool mouth kissed her flushed cheek. She started with fright and recoiled from the very thing she had been yearning for. She went hot and cold by turns, and to her horror perceived that he was laughing at her. Her stricken countenance made him laugh even more as he challenged, 'Is not that what you wanted, minx? Come now, confess it, you have been palpitating with desire ever since we left the house.'

'Oh! Oh!' She covered her face with her hands and burst into tears in earnest. Rather tardily, he took pity on her extreme youth and placed an arm about her shoulders, exerting a gentle pressure to hold her against him. 'Miss Branson, you have today learned a valuable lesson which will stand you in good stead in your future dealings with gentlemen.'

'Lesson?' The word was repeated dolefully as she fumbled for her handkerchief.

Idly, he began to toy with the tiny curls prettily decorating the nape of her neck. He felt her shiver under his touch and realised with no little surprise that he was arousing in her an ardour which inexperience could not keep in check.

This conclusion quickly sounded a note of caution. Little Ann Branson would not be the first young girl to trap a man into marriage by the oldest trick in the world. Somewhat peremptorily he withdrew his arm and said, as kindly as he could, 'Never let a gentleman see that you are interested in him, sweetheart. If a gentleman takes your fancy, always remain aloof, and let him chase you until he is so hot for...' Prudently, Richard bit back the words which hovered on the tip of his tongue and substituted, 'until he is so worn out with the chase that he lies at your feet like a beaten dog and begs you to have mercy on him.'

Ann blew her nose and sneaked a glance at her companion to make sure that he was not still teasing her. 'Mama often says that I must learn to curb my impetuous nature.'

The prim little phrase amused him. Still sensing, however, that he had set light to a train of gunpowder, he did not allow his amusement to show, and deliberately permitted a note of severity to enter his voice. 'Be a child a little longer, Ann. Marriage and child-bearing will come all too quickly.'

Richard felt very virtuous as he said this. For once he was behaving like a gentleman. Ann smiled uncertainly and placed a tentative hand on his arm. 'Shall you marry one day, Mr Darker?'

'I daresay I shall,' came the careless reply. 'When the right woman comes along.'

He did not add that the right woman must of necessity bring with her a considerable fortune to engage his attentions.

His heart stirred briefly at the sight of those vulnerable brown eyes gazing up into his face as though he held the key to all her future happiness. She really was dashed good-looking. Despite his noble intentions, Richard's gaze was lowered to assess the degree of roundness her figure would achieve when it reached maturity in two or three years' time.

When he raised his eyes to her face once more she was blushing furiously. Before he could stop himself he had kissed her long and lingeringly on the mouth, and though he permitted himself no further liberties, he could not escape the feeling that he had once more become needlessly involved in an unpredictable situation, the good or evil of which only time would reveal.

In the centre of the maze, where the grass grew thick and springy, and felt as smooth as velvet to the touch, Sophie Darker and young Harry Lambton lay on the ground together, the one giggling helplessly, the other red with fury as he accused, 'You are a teasing jade, Sophie. You twist a fellow's guts into knots and then refuse to pleasure him.'

Sophie sprang to her feet and stood

over the dishevelled Harry, who scowled fiercely up at her, all desire banished by the boiling anger inside him. Planting her foot, shod in its impertinent red shoe, on Harry's stomach, she said, with as much indignation as she could muster, 'And you, sir, are coarse and vulgar to suggest that I should *pleasure* you like one of your Haymarket whores.'

'Because you behave like one,' muttered Harry, and was rewarded by a painful jab of her heel in the region of his solar plexus which produced from him a yowl of protest.

Ignoring a string of ungentlemanlike curses, Sophie demanded suddenly, 'Did Clarissa *pleasure* you? You were mighty taken up with her last summer.'

A slow, tantalising grin slowly spread itself across the young man's face. 'Wouldn't you like to know, Miss Inquisitive?'

Sophie dug her heel in again. 'I'd lay wager you did not. She is too virtuous.' A thought struck her. 'Did you ask Sir Charles for Clarissa's hand?'

'Mind your business!' he snapped.

She laughed softly, pleased by his embarrassment. 'You would not have dared. You will have to marry some horse-faced, bandy-legged old maid with a fortune of ten thousand pounds a year, who will not mind paying your gaming debts.'

A moment later Sophie let out a shriek of fright as Harry seized her ankle, gave it a savage twist, and pulled her down on top of him. 'You bitch!'

He started to fumble at her clothes, but she tore herself from his grasp and rolled away from him. Like an angry cat she spat her defiance. 'Do not dare to touch me, sir, or you will smoke for it!'

He sat up, leaning on one elbow, and regarded her with a mixture of contempt and disbelief. 'You are mighty quick to change your mind. Who was it, pray, who suggested that we "take a stroll in the maze? See if you can catch me!"' he mimicked, coming astonishingly close to her high, clear treble, with its hint of shrillness. 'You were hot as a mare in season.'

Rage at her rejection of him made Harry deliberately vulgar in his choice of words. Her reply to these insulting remarks was absurdly formal. 'I was labouring under the mistaken belief that you were a gentleman!'

'So I am,' he retorted, 'and will one day

marry a lady a great deal more beautiful, and with a bigger dowry than your farmer brother could afford.'

'If you do not get transported to Australia first.'

Harry was on his feet now, rearranging his disordered attire and brushing away specks of grass from his breeches. He ceased these housewifely operations to stare at her, his lean, handsome face alert and watchful. 'What do you mean by that?'

She chewed childishly on her fingers and stared back challengingly. 'The revenue men would like to know about that cargo of French brandy you brought in last Friday night.'

'Cornelius was with me.'

'If the revenue men made inquiries, William would swear that Cornelius was at home that night...and so should I, but I might add that I'd seen you loading up a pony or two down by Witham Cove.'

'And what would a well-brought-up young miss like yourself be doing down at Witham Cove in the early hours of the morning?' he flashed back.

She giggled. 'Taking the air. I could not sleep.'

He knew by her manner and the way

she smiled lazily up at him that her threats were idly spoken. Nevertheless, she aroused in him a sudden feeling of revulsion, reminding him of a treacherous dog that will take meat from a human hand with apparent docility, and then will turn and bite that same hand when it is stretched forth to offer a caress. Like the dog, he must treat her with caution, though nothing could make him believe that William Darker would ever betray him.

'Let us go and get something to eat,' he suggested smilingly, and offered her his arm. With a look of sly triumph, she accepted the gesture of courtesy.

Dr Westlake, mellowed by several glasses of fine claret, led Patience Pochin out for the gavotte and was pleasantly surprised by the grace and vivacity with which she performed the intricate figures of the dance. The warm glow spreading from his stomach and reaching out in long tentacles to his furthest extremities, seemed to enhance the physician's powers of observation and he noticed, with newly-awakened eyes, the shining luxuriance of his partner's hair, dressed in the Grecian style, the fine quality of the lace adorning her gown of cream silk, and the fan of painted chicken skin hanging by a silver thread from her wrist.

Robert Westlake, absorbing with a gratified eye all these intriguing little details, began to wonder whether perhaps Miss Patience was possessed of a private fortune of which he had no knowledge. This notion was instantly dispelled by the realisation that a girl of Patience Pochin's grace and charm would not willingly surrender herself to the role of governess and companion, thrust upon her by the Darker family in return for food and shelter, and the vague hope that a gentleman in the county would be reckless enough to overlook her lack of fortune, if some pressing pecuniary need had not forced her to do so. How had the words grace and charm come into his head? He stared into the flushed face a little below his own, as though seeking to diagnose some rare and puzzling disease. Yes, by gad, she *was* graceful and charming...but not, alas, rich. Not even modestly well endowed. On the other hand, mused the physician, would he be able to endure a plain wife, even if she were possessed of a fortune? He was a man of fastidious tastes, and might find it almost impossible to lie with a slack-breasted female, to whose anatomical deficiencies he would almost certainly apply derogatory medical terms, even as he snuffed out the candles. The physician felt sure that under that beautiful gown, very close to him now as she twisted under his arm, there lurked a body so white and curvaceous as to send a man half out of his wits with desire.

Patience was regarding him a trifle quizzically. 'Doctor Westlake, your gaze is extremely searching. Do you find me wanting in some respect?'

Jerked out of his reverie, her partner smothered his confusion with a laugh. 'Indeed, Miss Pochin, your appearance lacks nothing at all. On the contrary, I was thinking that there is not a woman here today who can match you for looks and style.'

She was unmistakably pleased by the compliment. Her cheeks pinkened and she smiled. He noticed how white her teeth were. 'Forgive me, Miss Pochin,' he began hesitantly, as the dance ended and they moved together to the side of the saloon. 'It is none of my business, and please tell me to desist if I offend you, but is it your intention to remain long at Frinton Park?'

He thought her looks a little crestfallen as she answered, 'I shall stay for as long as Mr Darker finds my presence agreeable, and Miss Darker continues to require my companionship.'

He led her to a sofa near the buffet table, a small oasis of privacy in the crowded saloon, waiting until they were both seated before remarking, 'It cannot be too long before Miss Darker finds herself a husband.'

Patience's eyes were averted, glued to the clasped hands in her lap. 'I fear that Miss Darker is a very immature young person. In my opinion, it will be at least two years before she is ready for marriage.'

'A difficult young woman,' he murmured with a smile.

She looked up sharply, the dawning of hope in her eyes. It was the first indication she had had that Dr Westlake was not responding to Sophie's attempts to ensnare him. The physician, perhaps regretting his moment of indiscretion, said brightly, 'You must have been a great comfort to Miss Darker since the death of her mother.'

His companion shrugged slightly. 'Sophie is a very self-sufficient young woman. I believe she requires only that I shall be a good listener and run errands for her when her maid is not available to do so.'

Robert Westlake wondered whether he had imagined the note of bitterness in Miss Pochin's voice. 'You have done her very much good,' he comforted. 'For one who professes to dislike weddings she is in excellent spirits today.'

Patience, fearing that the conversation might begin to centre permanently around her charge, ventured to change the subject, and made bold to ask if the physician had lately added any interesting items to his collection of books. She reddened and went pale by turns when, in answer to the prim inquiry, he leaned towards her, and with an expression of great earnestness, declared that he would be the most miserable man alive if she should ever go away. Her hand flew to her cheek. It was like testing the heat of a flat-iron. She could have sworn that had she wet her finger she would have heard a faint sizzling noise. 'Oh, I do not mean to go just yet...'

In his slightly befuddled state, it seemed to the physician that her embarrassment somehow gave her an air of extreme frailty which boosted his masculine ego to the point where he had an overwhelming desire to protect her. He reached across to take her hand and pressed it to his lips. 'You must come and take tea with me, Miss Pochin, and I will show you my collection of books.'

Patience Pochin was left in that unenviable state of uncertainty which follows upon a daring proposition couched in wretchedly ambiguous terms. Had she or had she not received a proposal of marriage?

The thing that frightened Clarissa most as she mounted the little oak step-ladder and slid into the big curtained bed to wait for William, was not the prospect of the physical consummation shortly to take place, but that this act of intimacy would be conducted between two people who knew so little of each other's thoughts and feelings. Her relations with William Darker so far could scarcely be termed friendly, let alone intimate. Intercourse between them had existed on a plane of polite formality, combined, on his part, with a forced and sometimes slightly exaggerated jocularity which made her want to shrink to the size of a flea and hop away to freedom. She had tried once to convey to him, as tactfully as possible, that she did not care for fulsome compliments. After directing at her a look of stunned surprise he had responded to her plea by talking at a great rate through dinner about his farm, his horses and his various business interests until her brain reeled.

Despite his apparent disinclination to show her the less reserved side of his nature, however, she did not believe Mr Darker to be implacably cold or unkind. Nor did she think that he would employ the marriage-bond to use her ill, but in her attempts to assess the essential nature of his character she could not escape the conclusion that Frances Lacey had been the love of his life, and that Clarissa Branson could never be anything more to him than a poor second best. He was not going to permit himself to love her. She was to be used, like one of his fine brood mares, for the purposes of reproduction.

Where her own interests were concerned it was perhaps fortunate that the gentle-natured Clarissa was of a philosophical turn of mind. She had long accepted the fact that her niche in life would be decided upon by her father and mother and that she might, in the interests of financial gain, be called upon to marry a stranger. Mere acceptance, however, did not mean that her keen intellect could ignore certain arguments to be levelled against this arbitrary disposal of women in marriage.

Clarissa thought a great deal about social injustices and the right of women to strive for the pursuit of happiness. Long and hot were the arguments she had put forward on behalf of others, but she knew that had she been as vigorous in defence of her own rights she would have caused her parents much unhappiness, and this she was not prepared to do.

Wakeful and increasingly apprehensive in the unfamiliar bed, Clarissa remembered her mother's well-meant words of advice. 'Do not presume to dispute Mr Darker's wishes, my dear. Gentlemen usually know best about everything.' Did they? wondered Clarissa. Was it really true that their brains were larger, more superior in every respect to those belonging to the female of the species? Like many women of her time, Clarissa, though irritated by the subservient role forced on women by society, was not quite ready to burst forth from her bonds; the seeds of rebellion were there, nevertheless, germinating slowly, until the tender shoots could be passed on to the next generation.

Fifteen minutes after getting into bed Clarissa fell asleep. When at last he came, William had considerable difficulty in shaking her awake.

8

London Town

Clarissa's wedding-tour was not uneventful. The stay in London, which lasted a month, included a visit to Drury Lane Theatre to see Mr Garrick's famous portrayal of *King Lear,* concerts at the Rotunda Gardens, with William fidgeting beside his wife and emitting lengthy sighs of impatience, and dinner with Sir Joshua Reynolds, whom William commissioned to paint Clarissa's portrait.

One Sunday they drove down to Windsor in a hired carriage to watch the Royal

Family strolling in the Great Park. With other ladies Clarissa made her curtsey to Queen Charlotte, who walked by with a clutch of pale-faced, long-nosed ladies and stretched her extraordinarily ugly mouth into a condescending smile which embraced all, while it was directed specifically at none. The children of the King and Queen scampered by, chased by harassed young nursemaids, the latter endeavouring in vain to marshal them into a neat formation of three and two. Clarissa counted four boys and a girl.

'The King already has a great many children,' she remarked wonderingly.

William laughed briefly. 'It does not take much wit to beget a child.'

She sneaked a curious, sideways glance at this big, taciturn man who now escorted her everywhere. She had not yet become used to the idea that he was a permanent feature of her life. After three weeks of marriage he was still a stranger to her, a courteous, fairly considerate stranger, who snuffed out the candles before fumbling at the hem of her night-gown and doing what was necessary to ensure the continuation of his line. Clarissa was neither repelled nor pleased by her husband's attentions. She acknowledged only a vague, slightly disturbing sensation that there was something missing in this most intimate part of their relationship which she was either too stupid or too inexperienced to perceive. She placed her trust in time to reveal the truth to her.

It was a whole week before William went down to Haydon's Wharf at London Bridge to see Captain Gomez of the *Arethusa.* The good captain, brisk and business-like as ever, reported the death of four slaves on the homeward voyage, two men, one woman and a child, a very satisfactory state of affairs, due without doubt to the favourable weather conditions which had prevailed throughout the smooth and uneventful passage.
‘’Tis time they was sold off, though, sir,’ the Captain warned William. ‘some of ’em do ’ave the scurvy. We ran out o’ vittles two days afore we put into port. Them blackies ain't ’ad much to eat since we docked a fortnight since. Ain't got no stamina, that be the trouble. There's one o’ the females nursin’ a brat, but she run dry two days ago and...’

‘Yes, yes, *all right...*’ William interrupted

him testily. 'I shall see the factor today. We can arrange a sale at Rotherhithe tomorrow, or on Wednesday at the latest. Has my agent paid off the men?'

'Aye, sir.' Captain Gomez, a raven-haired, Devon-bred man, whose Spanish forebear had struggled ashore in 1588 off a wrecked galleon of Philip of Spain's invincible Armada, spoke with a weird blend of East London and Devon in his tones. He shuffled his feat uneasily and appeared reluctant to take his leave.

'Tomorrow then,' William said briskly. 'After the sale we can discuss the next voyage over a noggin.'

'Sir!'

'Yes, what is it?'

'Sir,' began Gomez diffidently, 'the slaves...'

'Yes?' William's voice now held a note of impatience.

'I 'ad to pay double for 'em,' blurted the Captain.

'Double!' William was outraged.

The Captain hastened to explain, his indignation matching his master's ''Tis them blackie chiefs, sir. They knows the value of what they do 'ave now. That old bas...begging your pardon, sir, I mean old

Daddy Jones on Martinique, 'e sold me two uv 'is wives what 'e's got no more use for. One cost more than t'other 'cos she's breedin'. Daddy said 'e couldn't let me 'ave two for the price o' one, even if she is breedin' a girl.'

A sardonic quirk of one eyebrow indicated William's surprise. 'How does he know that?'

Captain Gomez shrugged. 'Witch-doctor told 'im, most like. Cheeky varmint said I'd 'ave to take the risk o' the baby dyin'.'

'Hmm.' William pulled thoughtfully at his underlip. 'What with that thieving old rogue and this new Abolitionist movement that's afoot, we shall soon be put out of business altogether.' He dismissed the Captain with a wave of his hand. 'I'll see you tomorrow.'

'Sir?'

'What now?'

'Sir,' Captain Gomez touched his hat and ventured with an unworthy gleam in his eye, 'do we be goin' to 'ave a scramble at the sale, or do we be goin' to sell 'em off separate?'

'Separately,' William answered firmly, much to the Captain's disappointment. 'I am looking for something special and have no intention of seeing my own property snatched from under my nose before I get time to warn the auctioneer.'

The Captain, unwilling to submit without a struggle, said regretfully, 'I do love a scramble, sir. How them blackies do yell when the bell goes, and how they do fight to git away when they'm grabbed by them as wants to buy 'em.' The gleam in the Captain's eye was now positively flashing with fervour. 'Best way, reely, sir, if we do 'ave a scramble. There's 'igher prices paid when two buyers is fightin' over one black. I seen the price of a buck go up to a 'undred guineas at a scramble, as much as a gentleman'd pay for a good 'orse!' Small bubbles of saliva were now plainly visible at the corners of the Captain's mouth. He went on eagerly, 'I can grab what you'm after, sir, 'specially if 'tis a female. They don't stand no chance wi' me. I...'

'We shall sell them separately, Captain!' bawled William, and was gone before the Captain's mouth was closed.

Clarissa, although she found the prospect distinctly abhorrent, agreed to attend the slave sale, reasoning in her usual honest fashion that if one meant to champion causes, one should know what they were all about. William, still in happy ignorance of his wife's feelings in relation to slavery, hinted that there might be a surprise in store for her.

On the day of the sale a steady stream of people seemed to be making its way to the docks at Rotherhithe, and progress along the crowded traffic lanes was necessarily slow. The broad back of the Darker's coachman remained imperturbably unmoved as William addressed it in vehement tones to 'Get along, man, can't you? We haven't got all day!'

Clarissa bit back a remonstrance directed at her husband's unwarrantable irritation. She really did not know him well enough to gauge just how he would take a reproof, especially from the lips of a woman. Impudent, grinning faces appeared at the windows of the coach now and then, as inquisitive pedestrians jumped up and down to see who was travelling in such a smart turn-out. William glared at these plebeian invaders of his privacy, while Clarissa wisely resisted the impulse to laugh as a small boy thumbed his nose at her.

They arrived at last and, having alighted from the coach, pushed their way through the crowd pressing round the auctioneer's stand, William loudly proclaiming his status as slave-dealer to achieve a favoured position at the front.

Above the heads of the crowd Clarissa could see a forest of masts, decked with gaily coloured flags which denoted the country of origin of each ship. William nudged her and pointed at a tall warship with chequered sides painted in yellow and black. 'That is the *Coventry,*' he told his wife. 'She was built at Buckler's Hard on the Beaulieu River from good New Forest oak. Isn't she a beauty?'

Staring at the vessel's long, slender hull and soaring masts, Clarissa could not but agree, but she wished that she could have seen her with every stitch of canvas set sailing the open seas. Silent and still in the dock, with her sails furled and her upper spars dismantled she looked somehow forlorn and abandoned. It was difficult to imagine her teeming with life, her guns blazing away at the enemies of her country.

Clarissa was brought back to the present by the shouts of a woman selling meat pies and oranges. She clung nervously to William's arm, not liking the hard angularity of careless elbows jabbing at her sides, nor the mysterious and indefinable odours which filled her nostrils. She sprang from a section of society where body odours were masked by heavy and expensive perfumes, made all the more necessary by an ever-growing intercourse between upper-class families. Clarissa was having her first taste of the working classes gathered, en masse, to witness the spectacle of their own kind being sold like chattels, an entertainment which engendered only a little less exuberance than a public hanging or a bear-baiting.

The sale had already begun, and at that very moment two bucks were being led away by their new owners, hands still manacled, eyes downcast. Clarissa's heart stirred to pity and indignation, but she saw no pity in the faces surrounding her, only a kind of eager curiosity, and a complacent sense of superiority over these poor wretches who had been torn from their native soil and thrust among alien, pale-faced people who understood them not at all.

A young woman was put up next.

Handled familiarly by the auctioneer's assistant, who exposed her breasts as though displaying a pair of prize exhibits at a fair, she showed no sign of embarrassment, not even when the man ran his hand over her brown skin and winked at the crowd.

'She looks sullen,' commented William, casting an expert eye over the woman and fanning himself with his hat. 'She will not work well.'

'Who will buy her, then?' Clarissa asked.

William shrugged. 'A lady who needs a kitchen-maid, perhaps. She is not much good for anything else. Too thin and mean-looking to be a lady's-maid, or to wait at table.'

His wife gave an involuntary exclamation of regret, causing him to look down at her in surprise. 'Do not waste your sympathy upon such creatures. They are a heathen, unlettered race and can only derive benefit from serving among the civilised peoples of this island.'

Eventually, the woman was knocked down, after a great deal of energetic percussion on the part of the auctioneer, to an elderly gentleman in frock-coat and wig, who bore her off at such a rate that the crowd jeered and cat-called after him until he was out of sight.

'Kitchen-maid!' scoffed Clarissa. 'Poor thing. That odious old man wants her for a doxy.'

'She could do worse,' countered William, rather put out of contenance by the expression of such forthright views.

She could not resist teasing him a little. 'How shocking of me to perceive the obvious. I hope I have not forfeited your good opinion of me.'

He made a sound which signified neither pleasure nor disapproval and turned his attention once more to the auctioneer. Clarissa, whose head had begun to ache, and who desired only to get away from this depressing place as soon as possible, sensed a new alertness in him. She followed the direction of his glance which was now bent upon the stand. A young negress of about twenty or so stood submissively still while the auctioneer's assistant set about his business. Suddenly, William was no longer at Clarissa's side. He had moved to the foot of the wooden platform, and beckoning to the auctioneer said something which she could not hear. The man nodded, and the negress was removed at once from the stand. As she was led away she half-turned, resisting the rough grasp on her arm, and, straining to look over her shoulder, seemed fascinated by the sight of two very young children, a boy and a girl, who were being lifted on to the stand. So agonised was the young woman's expression that it took Clarissa but an instant to divine that she was the mother of these children. She caught a fleeting impression of rage and a kind of mad desperation before the negress was hustled away.

William, smiling broadly, returned to her side. 'That is settled, then. I think you will find her biddable enough.'

Clarissa's mouth dropped open. 'You did not...I did not want...' She broke off, intimidated by the look of cold resentment directed at her, then forced herself to go on. 'The children. They belong to her.'

His brows drew together in a black scowl of irritation. 'What children?'

'There!' She could hear her voice rising on a note of hysteria as she pointed frantically to the stand, where the babies had sat down and were drawing pictures in the dust at their feet, licking tiny forefingers to make an impression. William spared a glance for these innocent performers and a curious look of embarrassment crossed his face, as though he had suddenly discovered in himself a weakness he had not known existed. He hesitated for a fraction of a second before muttering, 'We cannot talk here,' then he seized Clarissa by the arm and dragged her towards the perimeter of the crowd. Unceremoniously he backed her up against the wall of a warehouse. His palms were placed flat against the wall on either side of her head as he said defensively, 'She is fortunate that I took her. With the brats at her heels some mill-owner from the north might have bought her and set them all to work spinning cotton. The children would have been dead within a year and the mother too, most likely.'

'But what will happen to the children now?' Clarissa persisted. 'They may still be bought by a mill-owner, may they not?'

William shook his head emphatically. 'Not without the mother to keep them quiet. They'll most likely be bought for pets.'

'Pets!' Clarissa almost shrieked the word, then blushed furiously at her own vehemence.

'Yes,' he confirmed sharply. 'As playmates for an only child, or something of the sort. For God's sake, ma'am, will you have done now? These creatures are none of your affair.'

'I do not want her. I do not want that *creature* you have secured for me,' Clarissa said stubbornly. She was close to tears.

His face tightened. Again she had the strange feeling that something waited to spring out at her from behind those clear grey eyes of his, something greatly to be feared...if one were guilty, that is. Now what on earth had put that thought into her head?

'Sophie can have her, then,' he decided abruptly.

'No!' The exclamation was dragged from Clarissa by the thought of the wretched woman's unhappiness being further increased by Sophie's selfishness and lack of consideration for others. She forced herself to speak more quietly. 'I will take her,

William, and thank you. She will do very well.' So saying, Clarissa ducked out from under her husband's imprisoning arms and made to turn away.

'Ma'am, come back here!' she was loudly commanded. Under the amused scrutiny of grinning bystanders she obeyed him, feeling very foolish, and was requested please to return to their lodgings alone, as he had business to attend to which did not concern her.

For the remainder of her wedding-tour Clarissa stayed deliberately submissive, agreeing with everything that her husband said, and doing her best to anticipate his needs. Her efforts were rewarded by seeing him relax in her presence, but not sufficiently to make her think that she was anything more than a necessary adjunct to his life.

After leaving London, they visited relatives at Hamfeld and Witham. By the time they arrived back at Frinton Park, in the middle of June, Clarissa had begun to suspect that she was with child. Perhaps because she knew it meant so much to William, some perverse need to punish him for his lack of interest in her prompted her to keep the knowledge to herself.

9

Richard Darker In A Quandary

'There is nothing in the world to prevent us from getting married,' Caroline Aynge said coolly, 'except certain reservations on your part which force you to the conclusion that you might do very much better than attach yourself for life to a widow with a fortune of five hundred pounds per annum.' The mild irony of her tone, belied by the cold stare of her hazel eyes, gave Caroline an uncharacteristically severe look as she addressed her lover, who reclined in an indolent sprawl upon the chaise-longue, apparently engrossed in the reading of various items of news in the London sheets.

'The truth, my dear Richard,' Caroline persisted quietly, 'is that you do not love me.'

With an exaggerated sigh the young man thus accused laid aside his newspaper and, swinging his booted feet to the floor, sat facing her with both hands gripping his knees. 'I see that you are determined to quarrel with me, my dear.'

'No, no.' she shook her head, looking distressed. 'It is merely that I have a woman's natural desire to be settled in life, to have children, and to look forward to a future which holds some security.'

His regard was frankly incredulous. 'Your future is secure enough. No woman is going to starve on five hundred pounds per annum.'

Again she shook her head, her large eyes filling with tears. 'It is cruel of you, Richard, to dissemble. Pray, do not make pretence that you do not understand me. I mean, as you very well know, the security which comes from the companionship and love of a husband and children. The security of being loved for myself, and not for any pecuniary advantage.'

In that moment Richard thought he knew how a cornered fox must feel. There really was no way out of this mess if he did not wish to forfeit for ever her good opinion of him. He had enough insight into his own character to know that it was her beauty which held him in thrall. The thought of another man caressing that blue-black hair, or running a finger down the porcelain perfection of her cheek, or clinging to that soft, yielding mouth, was almost more than he could bear. He realised with a slight shock that time was running out. A decision regarding his relationship with Caroline Aynge must soon be taken, and it must be the right one, for if he gave her up he knew there could be no going back. She was too proud a creature ever to renew their liaison if he rejected her now.

She was gazing at him very earnestly, as if trying to guess his thoughts. Her next words proved that she was no mean prophetess. 'I believe that you have not forgiven your brother William for being the first-born. You would dearly love to have become the master of Frinton Park and the proud owner of all those acres.'

How well she knew him! She was hesitating briefly, warned perhaps by the sullen expression which had cast a shadow over his face, before rushing on, 'I sometimes think, Richard, that you harbour in your breast the hope that William will die childless, leaving the inheritance to you.'

This remarkable indictment did not

enrage him. He did not leap to his feet and hotly deny her intuitive divination of his inmost desires. Instead, he restored his feet to the chaise-longue and lay back, resting his head on the buttoned scroll and closing his eyes firmly against the truth. Now was the time to stay calm and unruffled. He must never let her see how near she had come to the truth, nor yet suspect that the child Frances Lacey had been carrying when she took the hedge at Ditchley Bottom was not William's, but the seed of his younger brother who envied him his inheritance. For Frances, the beloved of her husband, had been a promiscuous woman, who had loved often and lightly, and who had inspired such adoration in her paramours that none had ever revealed her secret. It had given him a bitter kind of satisfaction at the time to know that the child Frances carried, if it proved to be a boy, would inherit all that he had been denied. *His* child, not William's, would one day be the master of Frinton Park.

At the time he had questioned Frances as to how she could be sure of the paternity of her child. Not bothering to wrap up in tactful phrases the bald acknowledgement of her infidelity, she had raised her arched brows at him, and in that affected London drawl she always employed, countered with, 'Odd's fish, Dick, d'ye think I cannot count?'

Richard opened his eyes. Caroline sat with her head lowered, a frown of concentration on her brows as she studied her embroidery. She did not appear to be waiting for any comment from him upon her last remark, but sensing his appraisal of her, looked up, her eyes begging for understanding. He said, 'If my thoughts are as villainous as you suppose them to be, they will avail me little now. If you place any value upon the opinion of a mere male, I believe my sister-in-law to be with child.'

She could not hide the quick upsurge of elation that this intelligence produced. Her eyes gave her away. 'Has she said so?'

Her obvious delight made him smile. 'She does not need to. She has a certain look about her. I noticed it immediately she returned from the wedding-tour. She looks like Frances did when she...' He bit off his next words, which would have told her more than it was wise for her to know, and substituted, 'Frances seemed to grow calmer, less communicative, less inclined for company. Clarissa is like that now.'

'If she is with child, why does she not tell Mr Darker and the rest of the family? I take it she has not, since you appear to be wandering in the realm of speculation?'

Richard extracted a toothpick from his waistcoat pocket and began investigating his upper molars. 'Perhaps she has, and William is enjoying keeping us all in suspense.'

'I hardly think that likely. Mr Darker does not give one the impression that he is a man to indulge in light behaviour.'

'Not like *this* Mr Darker.' The remark was made with a teasing grin, but she did not respond in kind. Into the ensuing, rather prolonged silence, while she plied her needle with the dexterity born of a long association with the intricacies of petit-point, she let fall words which, by their very inappositeness, put him immediately on his guard. 'Ann Branson is a charming girl, is she not?'

'Is she?'

'Oh, you had not noticed?' Her voice rose perceptibly. 'You danced with her three times at the assembly ball last week, and monopolised her attention at Lady

Lambton's soirée, but you did not notice her looks.'

His frown expressed genuine puzzlement and a hint of ennui. 'If I may be permitted to say so, ma'am, your mood this afternoon is querulous and exceeding sharp. May I not dance and converse with the sister of my brother's wife without causing eyebrows to jump and tongues to wag? If you are capable of discerning the true nature of our relationship, it must be obvious to you that the child is dying of love for me, or imagines herself to be so. Her interest in me is, I assure you, not reciprocated.'

'She would bring you a larger fortune than I.'

He could not deny that money was of paramount importance to him. 'Mmm, that is true, but perhaps not large enough. She is the youngest of Branson's daughters.' The answer came glumly as he went on picking his teeth.

Thrusting aside her embroidery as if it were a dish-clout, Caroline leaned towards him. 'Dick, what is it that you want out of life?'

He eyed her abstractedly, apparently absorbed in his grooming. 'I do not know,' he admitted at last. 'Dammit, I do not *know*! Stop quizzing me, Caro. There is nothing puts me out of temper so quick as a nagging female.' With a small sound of disgust he returned the tooth-pick to his waistcoat pocket and, rising, walked over to the window, from whence he could look out upon Mr Clark's bakery, with its tempting array of mouth-watering cakes and pastries.

Standing with his back to her, he said, 'Perhaps I am not the marrying kind, Caroline. I sometimes think it would have been better if I had taken up William's offer to buy me a commission in the army. I could have lived by the sword then, with no roots to bind me to the soil, to this cursed, blessed stretch of Sussex which claws at my heart like a possessive woman.'

It came as no surprise to Richard that he could express himself with greater facility when he could not see the look on the face of his mistress, nor read the latent fear in her large, sorrowful eyes. 'Certainly I shall not be content to live in William's shadow,' he continued, 'taking of his charity, watching his children spring up around him, each one a reminder of my own inferior status. If only,' he murmured, half to himself, 'I could bear to tear myself away from this home I love too much. It acts upon me like a drug, stunning my senses into apathy.'

Wrenching himself away from his contemplation of the outside world, he spun on his heel and strode towards her. 'Caroline,' he pleaded, 'in my penniless state I am not likely to attract an heiress, but...but I...'

'Could do a great deal better than to take me.'

'Ann Branson...' he began desperately.

'Oh, dear God!' She covered her face with her hands. 'Do not tell me that I am in competition with a school-girl!' This agonised appeal drew forth no immediate response and her heart sank. She whispered, 'Richard, do you not find me less communicative of late, less inclined to converse?'

After what seemed to her a great length of time she uncovered her face to find him staring at her questioningly. 'Yes,' she said quietly, 'I am with child.' She added with an air of great dignity, 'If you do not want to marry me I shall go to my late husband's mother in London. She is a woman of infinite compassion.'

10

Clarissa Meets With Approval

At approximately the same time as the foregoing conversation was taking place, a superficially less emotive exchange was in progress between William and Clarissa, the latter having at last communicated to her husband the fact that she was with child.

'Well done!' William's exclamation was little short of jubilant. 'How long have you known?'

'Not long,' she prevaricated. 'It is so difficult to be absolutely certain.'

His eyes expressed concern. 'You must see Westlake if there is any doubt.'

She smiled, brushing the suggestion aside as superfluous. 'I saw him this morning when you were out of doors. He has confirmed my suspicions.'

'I am glad.' And he was, genuinely glad, and obviously pleased with her promptness in fulfilling the purpose for which he had married her. If only, she thought wistfully, he could be pleased for my sake, as well as for his own.

William had been in the act of sorting through the end-of-quarter bills, hunched over the elegant black lacquer escritoire, with its bronze medallions and rows of little drawers. Her news totally destroyed his concentration. He pushed the papers aside and rose to come to her side, lifting the skirts of his green frock-coat as he occupied the chair facing hers. There was in his steady regard a new gentleness, a new awareness of her as a person which sowed the seeds of hope in her heart. 'One thing,' he began gravely, 'one condition which I must impose upon you.'

Instantly, her guard went up, veiling the soft, green-grey eyes with a defensible wariness. 'What is that?'

'You must not ride "Bugle" until after you are safely delivered.' 'Bugle' was the stallion which Richard had given her.

The rigidity of her stare softened and she let out a little sigh. 'Is that all? He is too spirited for me, anyway. Tom Gander wants to train him for the race-course. I said he might...provided that I could obtain your permission to bet on him.'

His face split into relieved laughter. 'You

have my permission.'

'You should laugh more often, sir,' she told him with spontaneous gaiety. 'It makes you look quite handsome.'

He stared at her for a moment, and she felt sure that he was about to retreat within himself, as he so often did when he thought her remarks flighty. All he said was, 'That's as may be. If we have a son, I hope for his sake that he takes after you.'

The family and household were delighted at the news, all except Sophie, who retired to her room and later reported a pain which required the immediate services of Dr Westlake. For once, William ignored his sister's whining complaints and refused to summon the physician. Clarissa unwittingly made matters worse by expressing the fear that if Sophie's wishes were thwarted she might very well throw a fit of hysterics which would be upsetting for everybody. 'If she does,' William growled threateningly, 'I shall take great pleasure in slapping her out of them.' He relented slightly when a deathly-white Sophie came down to dinner and picked at her food with one hand pressed to her heart. 'If the pain has not gone by the morning, the physician shall come,' he promised, and was rewarded with a wan smile.

Clarissa, watching her sister-in-law closely, could see no signs of an elaborate pretence. The girl could hardly simulate that degree of pallor, and yet, she argued with herself, Sophie was in tolerably good spirits before she knew I was with child. William so often defended Sophie's behaviour on the grounds that she badly missed the guiding hand of a mother, and Clarissa was willing to concede that this lack could have an adverse effect upon one of a nervous disposition. She smiled across the table at Sophie, determined to make an effort to like the girl and to attempt, if that were possible, to take her dead mother's place.

Sophie smiled back, but the smile did not reach her eyes. She hates me, thought Clarissa, feeling suddenly depressed. She really hates me. Or was she only imagining the aura of menace surrounding her in this tiny, shocking moment of a summer evening?

Salome, the coloured girl—so named by her father, who had come under the dubious influence of Christian missionaries—was at Clarissa's elbow with the salad. Clarissa smiled up at her, remembering the strange way Salome had come into her life. The large, dark, melancholy eyes seemed sadder than usual, though the eternal patience of the member of a persecuted race was still there, matched by the calm competence with which her hands performed their allotted tasks. Salome expected nothing very good to come out of life, and it was this undemanding attitude which had called forth kindness from the white missus, or so she reasoned. For this small mercy Salome was grateful, a gratitude tinged with the unspoken contempt she felt for all white people, who demeaned only themselves by their calm assumption that they were the superior race.

Clarissa thought she knew why Salome was sad. On a sudden impulse she promised quietly, 'I shall do my very best to find your children for you.'

A flash of white teeth expressed the young woman's joy, and her normally steady hand shook very slightly as she forked chives, chopped carrots and lettuce on to Clarissa's porcelain dish.

The after-dinner talk to which Patience, seated next to Clarissa, contributed nothing at all, turned to the possibility of Turkey declaring war on Russia, and Richard surprised everyone except William by announcing that he was to take a commission in the 10th Hussars.

'Poor Mrs Aynge, she will miss you,' observed Sophie with ill-disguised malice.

'She is coming with me,' answered Richard shortly, and a trifle gloomily, Clarissa thought, despite the swift reaction to his sister's blatant attempt to provoke him. 'We are to be married in the parish church, and then we shall go to London for a week before I join my regiment.'

Outwardly, Clarissa offered her congratulations. Inwardly, she breathed a sigh of unmitigated relief. Richard Darker had never been right for the unsophisticated Ann, though the child would undoubtedly grieve at his marriage and subsequent departure. In any case, Clarissa reasoned, Sir Charles would never have approved of his youngest daughter's liaison with a known philanderer. She said aloud, 'I hope that you will both visit us, Richard...as often as your military duties permit.'

Tightly, he smiled his thanks, unfairly disliking her for her cool assumption that she had the right to say whether or no he might come into his own home. She did have that right, however, and it angered him to know it. After much soul-searching Richard had at last settled for a definite future, but he was still not sure that he had chosen the right path. The only thing which had tipped the scale in favour of Caroline Aynge and a career in the army was the strong likelihood that Clarissa would produce a clutch of children to oust his hopes for good. There was, too, the tempting possibility of acquiring booty should England declare war on any of her European neighbours. Booty could be turned into hard cash, and in this way his dream of becoming as big a land-owner as his eldest brother might be realised. Richard's spirits might have lifted had he been able to see into the very near future, when England's most precious colony of America would declare war and fight for her independence.

Sophie, a compulsive eater, had now started to peel a China orange. The long white candles in their silver sconces bent to a fleeting draught from the partly opened windows and cast flickering shadows over her thin, pale face, which still bore signs of a prolonged bout of weeping. Intent upon the harmless game of removing the peel in one long, curling piece, she allowed herself to become careless, 'Shall you take the *Lady Susan* to Dieppe this month, Cornelius? Tom Gander says we are in for a bout of stormy weather.'

There was a long, awkward moment of silence, during which Sophie bit her lip in savage self-abuse. Cornelius reddened like a girl and patted his lace cravat, darting a bright, furtive look at Clarissa as he did so. His sister-in-law smiled serenely at him and warned, 'You will have to take very great care, Cornelius. Tom is a good weather-prophet. It might be infinitely less pleasant to turn turtle in the English Channel than to be caught red-handed by the revenue men.'

Patience giggled, while Sophie, furious at herself for having committed such a breach of confidence, demanded angrily, 'Who told you?'

The insolent manner in which this question was flung at her annoyed Clarissa, who was becoming a shade bored by Sophie's persistently aggressive attitude. She answered with deliberate coolness, 'Do you imagine, Sophie, that I am a simpleton? There is enough tea and sugar, brandy and tobacco stored in this house to sink the *Coventry,* not to mention two kegs of Geneva in the kitchen pantry which Cook insists contain Kentish cider!' These words were accompanied by a slow, amused glance at her husband, whose broad features split into a grin of appreciation.

'Sir Charles...' Cornelius began diffidently...

'...shall know nothing from me,' said Clarissa firmly.

Cornelius breathed a sigh of relief. 'I thought for a moment that my very dear friend, Miss Branson, had been indiscreet, though that would have surprised me a great deal, for I perceived her to be a lady of infinite tact.'

Clarissa stared at him for a moment before bursting into laughter. 'You cannot mean...no, I cannot believe that Aunt Charlotte...?'

'She is also a very discerning lady.' Cornelius was laughing too. 'She has an excellent palate for a good French brandy.'

Merriment rippled round the eating-room like clear spring water. Clarissa could almost believe that her former fears were largely imaginary, based on nothing more tangible than feminine intuition, a commodity which she had never regarded as infallible. When the laughter had died away William, in expansive mood, proposed that an invitation be extended to the local gentry to attend a picnic, a sort of celebration in advance. His eye caught Clarissa's unmistakably indicating approval at her handling of a taut situation.

Two days before the proposed picnic Dr Westlake, sacrificing ambition on the altar of charm and beauty, proposed to Patience Pochin. The event was not altogether unexpected by the Darker family. In recent weeks the two had been seen together, often in the village, once or twice in Lewes, and Patience had blossomed from quiet good looks into radiant beauty. The physician, as might be suspected, had not forsaken his ardent desire to get on in the world. Lowly he might be, with an income too small to capture the daughter of a gentleman, but there was always the question of patronage to be considered. The post of personal physician to a belted earl might not be beyond his grasp if he could but convince a sufficient number of influential people that his medical skill was far beyond that which was normally to be expected of a mere country physician.

To everyone's amazement, Sophie took the news of her cousin's felicitous expectations with an apathetic shrug and a rather tarnished comment to the effect that 'some people never come to know their proper station in life'. If this was meant to humiliate Patience, it could hardly have been less successful. She performed her daily round in a positive ferment of delight, agreed to Sophie's lightest and most irresponsible whims, and exuded an aura of divine patience which made even William smile.

'Thanks be to God that Sophie has taken it so well,' he remarked to Clarissa. 'She has quite grown out of her childish infatuation for Westlake at last. I told you we should see the end of it soon, and an end to her hysterics.'

Clarissa, too, admitted to a feeling of relief, though hers was tempered with an underlying fear that perhaps Sophie had merely changed course, and would shock them all into awareness of her true feelings by some stupid act of revenge. She thought it strange that William showed so little interest in Dr Westlake's courtship of Patience. In a way, her husband could be regarded as standing 'in loco parentis' to his cousin. Might one not expect him to exercise a degree of chaperonage, such as he would certainly display if his sister were to become involved with a suitor? As far as Clarissa knew, Dr Westlake had approached Patience directly to make his proposal of marriage, not deeming it necessary to ask William's permission first.

Not a little disturbed by her own thoughts, Clarissa eventually gave up trying to work things out and thrust all unwelcome intrusions aside. Together with Salome she made lists of her requirements for the baby she so longed to hold in her arms. She was generous in her new-found happiness, and, true to her promise, asked her husband if he would make inquiries concerning the person who had bought the little black children, in order to ascertain if they were in good hands. This was as far as she dared go at present, but she had not despaired of persuading William to buy back the little ones, if that were possible, so that they could be reunited with their mother.

Meanwhile, Salome had sublimated some of her maternal instincts by taking under her wing Dido, the little Jamaican boy who ran errands for the ladies of the household, and bounded out to hold the horses every time a carriage drew up in the sweep. Salome told Dido the folk-lore tales of his native land and made sure that his person came into frequent contact with soap and water.

Surveying herself in the long cheval glass on the morning of the picnic, Clarissa observed to her husband that she was distinctly on the increase. William laughed at the absurdity of this statement and poked a finger at her sprigged muslin skirts. 'Petticoats,' he scoffed, 'layers and layers of petticoats and a deal of imagination.'

She said without thinking, 'Perhaps you will be able to love me a little when you hold our child in your arms.' Even as the words slipped off her tongue she felt herself go red. She stared at her husband's reflection in the mirror, saw him hesitate as he stared back at her, and was surprised to note that his colour, too, had heightened. Then he had risen abruptly and was striding away, shouting orders through the small ante-chamber that divided their two bedrooms, and urging his valet to hurry with his coat.

Clarissa sighed dispiritedly and addressed her own mournful reflection. 'My dear, you have said the wrong thing...again!'

11

The Picnic

It was a perfect day for a picnic. The sun shone with impartial liberality upon masters and servants alike as the noisy cavalcade of assorted vehicles rattled its way up the winding path leading to the very top of Piddingfold Down. Half the county was there, the ladies displaying the new muslin prints—the wonder of the Lancashire cotton mills—and twirling their parasols above gaily bonneted heads, the gentlemen spruce and neat in freshly powdered periwigs, and sporting billy-cock hats, blowing lustily upon every variety of wind instrument.

As the carriages drew to a halt the gentlemen leapt athletically to the ground and turned to assist the ladies, who squealed with unfeigned delight as ribbons and laces snapped in the crisp wind, and they remained for an instant ecstatically airborne in strong male arms before being deposited gently upon the lush green carpet of their open-air eating-room.

The servants, whose jubilation at being released from the confines of house and stable was scarcely dissipated one jot by the fact that they must still serve, busied themselves with the preparations for the picnic, the men unharnessing the horses and putting them out to graze, the girls, in frilled caps and snowy aprons, shrilly urging the kitchen boys to 'Get the hampers down, do. Hurry now!' The boys, regarded by the upper servants as the lowest form of country-house life, obeyed with alacrity, eager to get their hands on the smaller variety of pork and venison pasties which could be conveniently secreted inside breeches and coat linings.

It was a full hour before the contents of all the hampers were safely deployed upon the checked table-cloths, the more succulent delicacies protected by fine netting against the incursions of determined wasps. During this time the younger element exercised their muscles by playing at French cricket, while their elders lay flat upon their backs, contemplating the cloudless heavens. Conversation, for the moment, was practically non-existent. It required the stimulus of a full belly to set your average Englishman's tongue on the wag, and then every subject under the sun would be chewed upon, and every *raconteur* and bore would get his chance. The course of the day's events was pleasantly predictable.

Ann Branson, by dint of watching Richard Darker's every move, managed to secure his undivided attention as he was returning from a wooding expedition to the little ring of trees which crowned the hill. As he emerged from the cluster of larches, carrying a bundle of small branches and twigs, he saw her running towards him and cursed himself for falling so neatly into a trap. He would have taken evasive action, but it was too late; she was already upon him, tearfully coaxing him back into the shelter of the young trees. He followed her reluctantly, depositing the twigs on the ground and casting an anxious look over his shoulder at the revellers sprawled down the slope of the hill. To his immense relief, nobody appeared to be at all interested in anything more than their immediate surroundings, not even Caroline, whose bright yellow parasol lolled drunkenly beside her as she dispensed milk to the children from a metal can.

Ann was standing with her back to a tree. The childish sullenness of her down-turned mouth caused him only mild irritation. He had made his decision, gone beyond the brief fascination she had exercised over his constantly vacillating affections, and was eager now to embark upon the future which offered him the only chance of amassing some capital he was ever likely to get.

'Take me with you.' Her words, spoken with such chilling intensity, took him off guard.

'I cannot. You know that I am to...' Intuition suddenly took over and nudged him into considering the probability that her family, in a conspiracy of silence, were keeping from her, as long as possible, the knowledge that he was shortly to marry Caroline Aynge. She knew only that he was going away to join the army. He was certain of it. 'I cannot,' he repeated more firmly. 'The army is no life for a woman, shuffled from place to place in the wake of her husband, and never knowing if he will return alive from an engagement with his country's enemies.'

'But I *love* you!' she protested, and to his acute embarrassment came towards him and flung her arms round his neck. He took hold of her wrists and, disengaging her arms, pushed her away, more roughly than he had intended. Her stricken countenance reproached him, and his sense of irritation and futility increased. 'I could not make love to an infant scarce out of the cradle,' and, as she started to plead yet again, 'You *bore* me, Miss Ann.'

She started back, her mouth open in a round O of shock. 'Oh, oh, heavens, how I hate you!'

'Who but a moment since loved me!' he mocked.

'You are horrid, a beast, a...' She could not find words to describe his perfidy and took refuge in tears. He watched her for a second or two as she stood with her head bowed, fumbling desolately for her handkerchief. Then he turned on his heel, retrieved the bundle of twigs, and began a purposeful descent of the hill.

'I shall follow you!' she screamed after

him. 'You will not be rid of me so easily!'

The empty threat made him smile.

William, replete with good food and wine, admitted to feeling a little sleepy. 'Go to sleep, then,' encouraged Clarissa, 'but first put your hat over your face. The sun is very hot today.'

'What shall you do while your husband snores away the afternoon?'

She showed him a book. *'Hakluyt's Voyages to the West Indies,'* he read with surprise. 'I did not know that you were interested in voyages of discovery.'

She smiled and said lightly, 'Salome comes from the West Indies. I shall read the book aloud to her. One day, very soon I hope, Parliament will vote for the abolition of slavery. Salome will be free then. She may want to return to her home.'

'The day Salome and her kind go free, your husband, ma'am, will lose a goodly slice of his income,' he said with heavy sarcasm, 'the slice that keeps you in expensive gee-gaws.'

She was unrepentant. 'You can employ your ships to better purpose.'

'What better purpose? Name a more profitable trade than the buying and selling of heathens.'

'One day I shall convince you that it is wrong.'

'Mind your own business ma'am.'

But she was not to be put off by the brusqueness of his manner. 'I do not want my...our son to be a trafficker in human flesh.'

William refused to accept the challenge and abruptly changed the subject. 'You are not wearing the necklace I gave you. You haven't taken against it, have you?'

'Oh, yes...my necklace.' Clarissa's hand went to her throat. 'I could not find it in my jewel-case this morning. I think Salome must have put it in the drawer by mistake. It was getting late and I was in too much haste to look. It is not really suitable to wear at a picnic, you know.'

'I trust it is not lost,' he said without much concern. 'It cost me a hundred guineas.'

Clarissa tried to dismiss the small, nagging fear which had been cutting across her thoughts all the morning. She should have cut out her tongue, of course, before mentioning the mislaying of the necklace to

Sophie. The mischievous girl was bound to give the matter an airing.

Sophie smiled sweetly at Lady Lambton. 'Patience is very fortunate to be making such a good match. In her station of life it is not always easy to find a suitable partner, especially when one has no fortune.'

'No, indeed.' Lady Lambton's jaws clamped briskly on a slab of fruit cake, her rouged cheeks rotating clockwise as she avoided the side of her mouth which was toothless. Her little blue eyes surveyed Sophie with sharp curiosity. 'And when shall *you* take a husband, Miss?'

'Not until I find one who is very, very rich,' replied Sophie, sipping at her glass of Madeira.

'Hoity-toity!' Lady Lambton belched indelicately. 'My Harry will not do for you then?' Her unremarkable features bore an expression of fatuous indulgence. 'The rascal. He spends all his allowance on gaming at the tables and betting on race-horses with three legs.' She chuckled at her own wit.

'He must marry an heiress,' Sophie replied loftily. 'If she is plain enough she will pay all his debts for him, just to please.'

Lady Lambton bridled in defence of her favourite offspring. 'Harry will do well enough for himself. He is a handsome, loveable boy, and very like the King in appearance, I am told.'

Sophie, bored with this eulogizing of someone she had decided to despise and consider unworthy of her attentions, lapsed into silence. Harry Lambton had forfeited her regard when he had refused to wilt under her teasing. She had wanted him to grovel at her feet. Instead, he had shown her a clean pair of heels.

The garrulous Lady Lambton was soon off on another tack, namely Clarissa's interesting condition, expressing the hope that 'everything will go well this time for poor Mr Darker'.

'Clarissa will not fall off a horse, if that is what you mean,' returned Sophie unfeelingly. 'She don't ride enough for that.'

'And a very good thing too,' approved her companion, whose acquaintance with horses was limited to a couple of sleek backsides glimpsed through the windows of her carriage.

'Clarissa is not in good spirits today,' remarked Sophie, helping herself to some more Madeira. 'She has mislaid her diamond necklace.'

'Oh, how very provoking!' Lady Lambton threw up her hands in horror and immediately put the worst possible interpretation upon this information. 'You do not mean to say that it has been stolen?'

Sophie shrugged. 'We hope not, but one can never be sure of the servants.'

'That black creature?' suggested Lady Lambton. 'I do not like her. She has sly eyes.'

'I do not know.' Sophie was vague. 'We employ so many servants.'

Patience chose this moment to appear before them, cheeks aglow from her exertions with bat and ball. 'Come on, Sophie,' she invited gaily. 'We need a fourth to make up the game.'

The sight of so much exuberance was too much for Miss Darker. She observed her cousin's animated face and girlishly dishevelled hair with disfavour, and lying back upon the grass closed her eyes with a finality which effectively spurned any attempt at further persuasion. With a nervous smile at Lady Lambton, who could be forgiven for thinking her entirely unsuited to fill the role of chaperone to a young girl, Patience ran off in search of a more willing partner.

Harry Lambton, half-way up a wild apple tree in search of any prematurely ripe offerings, dropped a hard green object on to Cornelius's unsuspecting head and scrambled down to sit beside his friend. He emptied his bulging pockets and set his booty upon the ground beside him. 'Take one,' he invited.

Cornelius made a face. 'Too small and sour,' he opined. 'You'll give yourself a belly-ache.'

Undeterred by this warning, Harry bit into one of the apples, pridefully resisting the impulse to grimace horribly as the sour taste contracted his stomach muscles and forced the saliva into his mouth. Cornelius neighed with laughter. 'Draws your arse up through your belly, don't it?'

Harry, his bluff called, spat out the remnants of the apple disgustedly and ran his tongue round his dry teeth. 'You will have to take the *Lady Susan* over to Dieppe next week,' he said. 'We've got visitors coming to the house. Mama's brothers and their wives. A mighty curious bunch of Philistines from northern parts.'

Cornelius nodded assent. 'I meant to, anyway. I've a very special cargo coming.'

'Oh?' Harry pricked up his ears. 'What's afoot, then?'

Cornelius scrabbled around in his pocket and withdrew a letter which he passed over to his friend to read. 'From Mama's brother-in-law,' he explained. 'My Aunt Cassy married a Frenchman, a Count no less. This same nobleman is, as you will read, in some trouble with the authorities. He published a pamphlet deploring the plight of the French peasants and now reposes in the Bastille charged with high treason. Uncle Jean fears they might string him up, and he wants up to get the Countess Julie out of France *incognita* in case the powers that be vent their spite on her too.'

Harry, quickly perusing the letter while Cornelius was speaking, looked incredulous. 'Dam'me, Cornelius, you ain't risking your neck for some Froggie female ye don't even know?'

'She *is* my first cousin,' Cornelius pointed out reasonably. 'I must.'

'Yes,' agreed Harry doubtfully. 'I suppose

you've no choice. Let that be a lesson to ye, Cornelius. Never marry a woman with connections abroad.'

'I shall not marry at all if I can help it,' returned Cornelius with a delicate little shudder. 'Females spend most of their time exercising their jaws.' He added as an afterthought, 'I might have to, of course, if I am pressed for money. Then I shall find myself an heiress.'

'That is what I mean to do,' Harry said. 'It is the only way a gentleman can find any happiness in this life. If ye fall for beauty ye're a dead man.'

Gloomily, Cornelius concurred in this cynical philosophy. He asked idly, 'Are you thinking of asking for Sophie, then? William can raise a few thousand, I reckon.'

Harry was silent for so long after the posing of this question that Cornelius looked at him curiously. 'Have I said something out of turn?'

'No—o—o.' Harry was wondering how far Cornelius's loyalty to his family could be stretched. Since his neck might be similarly affected, he decided to take a chance, putting the matter as tactfully as he could. 'Would Sophie ever be unwise enough to rattle to the revenue men about our little business enterprises?'

Cornelius caught his meaning at once. 'Betray us, you mean?'

'Well, yes.' Harry was enormously relieved that the thin ice had not given way under him. Cornelius pondered the question, mindful of his sister's queer, secretive ways, her jealousy, her innate, distressing spitefulness towards others, notably her wretched cousin Patience, who, it seemed, was no longer so wretched and was about to find her wings. He said thoughtfully, 'She is pretty loyal as far as the family are concerned,' and then, with a flash of insight, 'You haven't upset her, have you?'

Harry looked confused before confessing miserably, 'I called her a teasing jade because she would not...well, dammit, Cornelius, she leads a man on so!'

Cornelius did not pass judgement. 'Perhaps it would be better if you did lie low for a bit,' he suggested. 'I passed a man on the Newporth turnpike road who had been strung up and left to rot. According to the warrant notice, he had been sentenced to death "for persisting in the illegal traffic of dutiable goods".'

12

Interlude

'Please, please do not,' she begged, and gave a little gasp of pain as his fingernails dug into her breasts and his groping hands squeezed her unlovingly.

'Please, please do not!' he mocked, and took her with a degree of animal savagery which indicated that he was in his cups. She lay under him, feeling her stomach heave, waiting, taut as a fiddle-string, until he rolled away from her, fumbling at his nether garments and swearing under his breath as laces and buckles eluded the grasp of his slack fingers.

With unsteady hands she laced up her bodice and tugged at her skirts. She was crying. He made a sound of irritation. 'For God's sake! For a bitch who could not wait to kick up her heels, you've become mighty nice all of a sudden.'

She struggled to get her voice under control. 'Why do you treat me so cruelly?

I have done nothing to cause you hurt.'

'You pleasure me,' he answered coarsely, 'and I do not give up my pleasures until I grow tired of them.'

Her head turned towards the dark, faceless silhouette beside her. 'I wonder that you can derive enjoyment from an unwilling woman.'

He gave a low chuckle. 'You were not so unwilling when you thought I might marry you.'

She fell silent while he completed the final adjustments to his clothing, then urged quickly, 'I beg you sir, to set me free. I cannot endure to come to you again in this way. You are turning me into a common whore.'

He was on his feet now and standing over her, legs astride her recumbent body. 'Nevertheless, you *will* endure, for as long as I care to make you, since if you do not, a word in the right ear will ensure that your matrimonial aspirations are blighted for ever.'

She stared up at the black shape looming over her, thankful that the object of her hatred was anonymous in the impenetrable, moonless night. 'I think I shall kill myself.'

His laughter sounded very loud in the velvet silence which enshrouded them. Only the thin hoot of an owl, calling from the blasted elm in Ditchley Bottom, sounded a mocking note of counterpoint to her distress.

'You'll not do that. The game has not yet run its course. When I chase a fox I know the exact moment he is going to give up, and you, my charming one, are a long way from surrender.'

'So I am one of your foxes, am I, to be run to the death?' The break in her voice belied this attempt at brave defiance. She saw the whiteness of his teeth as his lips drew back in a grin. 'A vixen, that's what you are, and I'll run you for as long as it pleases me.'

'When I am married…' she faltered, but before she could say any more he was gone, striding away down the hill, leaving her to weep among the tall grasses which bordered the field of wheat.

13

Cornelius and Richard Darker Encounter The Law

Cornelius ran the *Lady Susan* into Witham Cove, lowered the sail, and allowed her to drift in towards the beach. The revenue men had sharp ears for the sound of oars. The dark bulk of Richard's figure, muffled by cloak and hat, was clearly outlined against the lightening sky. 'Cutting it deuced fine,' Cornelius whispered. 'Is she awake yet?'

'Yes,' Richard whispered back, and, leaning down, assisted the stirring form of a woman to rise and sit on the damp thwart.

'Sommes-nous arrivé?' she queried. She sounded very frightened, her voice as light as a lark's trill.

'We are, *Madame,*' Richard assured her. 'In half an hour's time you will be within the shelter of our house.'

'C'est bon.' She shivered. *'Je fais froid.'*

Gallantly, Richard removed his cloak and placed it about the shoulders of the Countess, who thanked him with a smile, the coquetry of which was just discernible in the pale dawn light. Stiff-legged, the young woman struggled to her feet, and giving her hand to Cornelius, who was already in the water up to his knees, bravely plunged into the water and waded ashore.

Richard beached the dinghy and followed close on their heels, and the three crunched their way over the stones, the Countess stumbling now and again over the unfamiliar terrain. The smooth gravelled walks of her chateau near Paris had never prepared her for this. She did not complain. The shadow of the Bastille had lifted. The fate of her husband, now under sentence of death, would soon be forgotten in the comforting, candle-lit radiance of the London salons, as the gentlemen bowed over her tiny hand and admired the diamonds and rubies which she had so prudently rescued. *Madame la Comtesse* was very young.

The clandestine travellers were almost at the top of the steeply sloping path leading to the summit of the cliff when a shout from the beach below alerted them to the fact that they were discovered.

Cornelius, who had two one-gallon kegs of contraband brandy hidden under his cloak, shouted to his brother, 'Come on, Dick! Tom will have left the horses by the elm in Ditchley Bottom.'

Richard needed no second bidding, and after he had scrambled up the remaining few yards the three took to their heels along the path which led inland. The legs of the Countess quickly failed to support her. She turned her ankle painfully on a piece of rock and called to her rescuers that she could go no further. In response to her frantic appeals, Cornelius slowed down and, turning, waited for Richard to come pounding up. 'Give me the tobacco,' he said urgently. 'I will ride with the stuff to Miss Branson's cottage at Pysamber. This one is too close for comfort.'

Richard was already in the process of removing a leather belt from his waist. Hanging from it were several packets wrapped in waxed paper. It was a poor harvest, but the best they could have done under the circumstances, with the Countess as their prime consideration.

Cornelius took the belt and clipped it

round his own over-burdened waist. 'I feel like a pack pony,' he muttered. He cocked his head as the sounds of pursuit drew nearer. 'Take the Countess home, Dick. If they catch you they will find nothing on you, and there is no crime in bringing a lady from France.'

'They'll have spotted that there are three of us,' Richard pointed out as they set off again.

'Use your ingenuity, dear boy,' came Cornelius's unhelpful and rather breathless reply.

The horses were reached in safety and the fugitives were soon mounted and off, with the revenue men now hard on their heels. The latter, though forced to take their horses by a circuitous route to reach the cliff-top, had quickly caught up. Cornelius, adept at such exercises, gave them the slip by concealing himself and his animal in a clump of trees at the bend of the road. He watched them thunder by, whipping on their horses, and gave way to the laughter bubbling up inside him. Richard had wanted a bit of fun before he settled down to his wedded state. Damned if he wasn't going to get it. Still chuckling, Cornelius headed his mount towards Pysamber and the haven of Aunt Charlotte's cottage.

'Dearest boy, of course I shall look after your property for you. How very exciting!'

Miss Charlotte had at length answered Cornelius's repeated knockings upon her door and seemed totally unabashed to present herself, clad in night-gown and slippers, and with her hair in rag curlers. She ushered her unexpected visitor into the small parlour and fussed with the cushions on the sofa, urging Cornelius to 'Sit down, do, Mr Darker. How very tired you must be after your exertions.'

The laughter which had been threatening to overcome Cornelius ever since he had eluded the revenue man, now burst forth into a positive crack of sound, followed by harsh little staccato gasps which he was quite unable to control.

'Oh, dear...oh, deuce take it...' Cornelius at last managed to regain command of his features, and having mopped his streaming eyes with his handkerchief, exchanged glances with a merry-eyed Miss Charlotte, who had seated herself beside him. 'Dam'me, ma'am, if you ain't the spunkiest female I've set eyes on in a long time.'

He stood up, divesting himself of his cloak and revealing to her astonished gaze two kegs of good French brandy and the pouches containing the tobacco. He detached these articles from his person and deposited them on the floor. 'If you will be so kind as to look after these for a day or so, ma'am, I shall be very much obliged to you. I do not think the revenue men will come sniffing round here, bothering a highly respectable lady like yourself who has never been in trouble with the law.'

Miss Charlotte giggled. 'No, indeed.' She looked at the items scattered on the floor. 'I should not like to be discovered in an illegal act, you know. It would be so embarrassing for poor Charles.'

This reference to Sir Charles Branson reduced Cornelius to a proper sobriety. 'I am a thoughtless villain, ma'am. I should never have come here in the middle of the night, putting you to all this trouble.'

'Pooh!' She dismissed this nicety of feeling with a wave of her hand. 'Do not suppose that I am going back upon my word, sir. I meant what I said when I told you that you might count upon me as a friend in your little...er, your business dealings. My remark was made more as a reminder to myself that I must take proper precautions. These items shall be put in my cellar until you can call for them, and you may rest assured that it will take a bold fellow who will dare to insist upon a search there.'

'I believe you, ma'am,' said Cornelius, 'and here is something to repay your generosity.' So saying, he unwound a length of green Bussels brocade from his waist.

'Oh, Mr Darker! Oh, really, I declare!' She was overwhelmed by the gift. 'No,' she went on firmly, 'I could not take it. It is too great a recompense for such a trifling service.'

'Not trifling, ma'am, I assure you,' returned Cornelius with feeling. 'If the revenue men had caught me with this little lot on me they would have clapped me into Lewes gaol before I could wink an eye.' Seeing the look of doubt clouding Charlotte's face, and the obvious struggle taking place within her breast, Cornelius offered a sop to her conscience. 'A gentleman may not accept favours from a lady unless he is in a position to recompense her. I may want to throw myself upon your mercy again. How can I do that if you will not accept a small gift from me?'

She capitulated with a giggle. 'Well, then, thank you, Mr Darker. I shall make myself a gown for Richard's wedding.'

He batted one eyelid at her. 'I shall buy you some Ghent lace the very next time I am across the water.'

Her bright eyes crinkled into positive ecstasy. 'Shall you take a glass of brandy, Mr Darker?'

Cornelius looked down at the kegs, an expression of pained regret crossing his face. 'Ma'am, I should like nothing better than to broach one of these kegs, and that's the truth, but they have been promised to two of my best customers, and the profit for this night's work will be little enough as it is without drinkin' 'em.'

'No, no!' Charlotte was shaking her head. 'You do not understand me correctly, Mr Darker. Some of *my* brandy, I mean.' Having made this announcement with a coy little smile she went to a corner cupboard, and unlocking it with a key which she delved for in her work-basket, took down a brown flagon. She held it up for Cornelius's inspection. 'From the Armangnac region of France,' she informed him. 'I bought it from Mr Henry Lambton.

He is in your trade too, you know.'

Cornelius thought he'd choke he laughed so much.

When Cornelius Darker arrived home, just after six o'clock in the morning, he was surprised to spy Dr Westlake's phaeton drawn up before the front door and a flurry of coming and going among the servants in the hall. His first thought was that Clarissa had miscarried the baby, but then Clarissa herself came into the hall, and catching sight of her brother-in-law, flung herself upon him. 'Cornelius, such a dreadful thing has happened!'

'Sophie has a real pain,' he guessed, and immediately rejected his own flippant suggestion by a shake of the head. Clarissa would not get into such a taking over Sophie's vapours.

His second thoughts were quickly confirmed. 'No, not Sophie. It is Richard, and the lady he brought home with him.'

'What about them?' Cornelius was divesting himself of his cloak as he spoke and hurling it at a passing servant observed, 'Do not tell me that the revenue men caught up with them?'

Clarissa's eyes were black with shock. 'They shot at them, Cornelius! Richard is wounded in the arm and the lady...' She broke off, stuffing her clenched fist into her mouth. Tears ran down her cheeks.

'What?' Cornelius's voice rose a whole octave. 'Dammit, Clarissa, what?'

'She is dead, poor little thing,' sobbed Clarissa, and fell on his shoulder. Absent-mindedly, he patted her back, struggling with a complexity of thoughts. He could not believe it. It simply could not have happened. 'What the devil...?' He took Clarissa by the shoulders and pushing her from him, shook her gently. 'How did it happen?' he demanded harshly.

Clarissa wiped her eyes with the back of her hand, pulling herself together with an effort. The sorry tale poured out. 'Richard says that the revenue men gained on them a bit and shouted to them to stop. When they did not, they fired two volleys at them, hitting Richard in the arm and knocking the lady off her horse. At first, Richard thought she was only wounded like himself, but when he got off his horse and ran to her, he discovered that she was dying. He picked her up and held her in his arms while he let off a string of curses at the revenue men.'

'They do not commonly fire off their

pieces,' Cornelius put in quickly.

'No,' she agreed, 'but they had had orders to tonight...' Wearily, she corrected herself, '...last night. They told Richard that the justices are becoming alarmed at the quantity of smuggled goods finding their way inland from the south coast, and they consider it high time the smugglers were taught that the revenue men mean to catch them.'

'Someone must have informed on us,' Cornelius decided thoughtfully. Grim speculation narrowed his eyes. 'I wonder...? Is the saw-bones with Richard?'

She nodded. 'He says it is only a flesh wound, and that it will heal quite quickly.'

'And the Countess?'

Clarissa's eyes were startled as she gave a little shiver. 'Is...was she a titled lady? I did not know.'

Cornelius was embarrassed by the directness of his sister-in-law's candid stare. 'Yes, well, William thought it better not to say anything to anybody until it was all over.'

She said with unveiled sarcasm, 'Very prudent of him. Women are never to be trusted with secrets like that. They are such incredible rattlers, are they not?'

Cornelius looked like a schoolboy who has been caught netting geese, but Clarissa was not prepared to relent. She said distantly, 'The *lady* is in the blue bedroom. William says that as none of her husband's relatives are over here, we should try to contact them in France.' She paused, her eyes troubled. 'It is awkward...she is probably a Roman Catholic and must be buried according to the rites of her Church. William says she is to be coffined and put in the mausoleum until we hear from France, but we must have a priest. I believe they can administer the last rites if a person has not been dead for more than half an hour. I am afraid in this case...' Her voice tailed off.

'Yes, deuced tricky,' muttered Cornelius. He clenched his fists. 'If I thought that jealous jade...' He did not answer the large question-mark in Clarissa's eyes, but asked instead, 'Where is William?'

'With Richard and Dr Westlake.'

'Go and get some rest, Clarissa, you look done up,' he advised kindly, and before she could say any more was taking the stairs two at a time.

Sophie's chamber door was uncompromisingly closed against the early morning's unusual flurry of activity. Cornelius's mouth was set into a hard, unrelenting line as he knocked perfunctorily and without waiting for permission to enter, did so, striding towards the bed where his sister lay flat on her back, her eyes wide open. He sat down heavily on the side of the bed, eyeing Sophie with a faint air of dislike. She stared expressionlessly back at him. 'I suppose you know,' he began, 'that something untoward has occurred? Did it not prompt you, Miss, to find out what it was? Or perhaps you already guessed?'

She sat up in bed then, bony shoulders sticking through the thin stuff of her nightgown, which hung straight down over her non-existent breasts. 'What do you mean?'

'What do you mean?' he mimicked, disgust flaring in his eyes. 'I mean, Miss, that it is my belief you informed on us, only you thought that I was taking Harry Lambton with me tonight, and when you found out that it was Dick who was to go you took fright and hid yourself up here in your confounded green eyrie.' He looked about him, plainly despising her taste for *Chinoiserie.*

Her eyes were black with a mixture of fright and fury at this accusation. She pressed her back against the quilted headboard behind her, a small, fierce wild animal at bay, and spat defiance at him. 'I did not inform on you! I did not! Harry Lambton told me a week ago that he was not going with you on last night's run.'

The anger in her brother's eyes was replaced by doubt. Seeing it, she pleaded, 'Cornelius, you *know* I would not do anything to harm you!'

He did know it. Whatever had possessed him to think otherwise? Sophie was a mischievous piece of baggage, but she'd die to protect her own flesh and blood. 'Then who the devil...?' he muttered.

'Clarissa?' she suggested slyly, and received a stinging slap on the cheek for her pains.

'Ow! You monster, Cornelius!' She laid her hand against her burning face.

'Serves you right, Miss,' he returned unsympathetically. 'Clarissa is a lady. She would never betray us, and I'll not have you making your deceitful insinuations around the house. You keep your mouth shut about this night's business. It is just possible that no one informed on us at all, and that the revenue men turned up by sheer chance.'

'Likely!' she scoffed.

'Well, whoever it was, I shall find out,' he promised darkly, 'and he will pay, you may be sure of it.'

Cornelius, in spite of his womanish affectations, was all man when it came to a small matter of avenging himself upon an enemy.

14

Interlude

'It is murder!' she screamed, and he placed his hand over her mouth, though there was no one to hear her except a flock of black-headed gulls which keened upwards into the bright morning sky.

'A black!' he jeered. 'He was a slave. I have a right to do with him as I please.'

'And he had a right to be treated like a human being.'

'He was scum. Not worth one of my dogs.'

'Oh, you are despicable!'

He pushed her back roughly on the coarse grass and brought his face close to hers. 'You did not see anything.'

She said through clenched teeth. 'I saw you beat him till he could not stand because he had forgotten to groom your horse, and the following morning, when the slaves were sent out to work in the fields, he was missing.'

'You believe, like everyone else, that he died of a seizure.'

'I know what I saw!'

'You know what will happen if you tell anyone what you *think* you saw?'

'I do not care any more.'

He drew back, and she seized the opportunity to scramble to her feet. 'I do not care!' she repeated. He sprang at her, gripping her by the shoulders. 'You will keep a still tongue in that stupid head of yours if you do not want to make a fool of yourself. If you point the finger at me, people will call you a liar. I am much respected in this county.'

'The gentry of Sussex, it would seem, are not very particular about the company they keep.'

He chuckled softly. 'Is that the best you can do?'

'Oh, dear God, how I hate you!' Her clenched fists beat impotently at his chest, and the laughter sprang from his throat as he caught her wrists in a grip of steel. With a savage twist which sent the hot pain coursing up her arm, he flung her to the ground again. Her cries of protest were lost among the rush of sound through the trees and the squeaky chatter of small diurnal wild animals.

15

Patience Pochin Goes Shopping

Patience, whose marriage was to take place from Piddingfold parish church on the last day of August, now spent a large portion of her time in Mr Smith's Emporium in the High Street of Piddingfold village, purchasing certain articles which were absolutely indispensable to the requirements of a bride, such as gloves, handkerchiefs, ribbons, lace trimmings and feathers.

On some of these expeditions Patience was accompanied by Sophie, who, tempted by Mr Smith's delectable display of feathered bonnets and gay, ivory-handled parasols from France, spent her allowance with a prodigality which made Patience wince. It would have taken a great deal more than Sophie's extravagance, however, to spoil her cousin's eagerness to possess all those items which did not stretch her own meagre purse to bursting-point, and she discovered that she could view without particular envy her wealthy relative's incursions into the realms of figured satin and Lyons silk, while remaining perfectly content with muslins and cottons.

Patience always asked Clarissa's permission before making her forays into the village, thus underlining her dependent, semi-servile status. Clarissa, whose complacency grew and even out-paced her increasing girth, raised no objections to the frequent outings, and expressed a considerable degree of interest in the contents of each pink-wrapped package, an abundance of which swayed about Miss Pochin's person like corks on a tinker's hat.

One hot, windless afternoon in early August, Patience, having decided that a silver-beaded reticule was an essential requisite for her trousseau, persuaded an indolent Sophie to accompany her, and the two set off together to walk the three miles to the village. Sophie would have preferred to take the gig, but Patience, with a maddening and newly-acquired air of authority, declared that the walk would do them both good. She received for answer only a sharp, definitive click as Sophie snapped open her parasol.

Patience used the occasion to instruct, employing a questions-and-answers system which was the approved method of educating young ladies in the late eighteen century. It went something like this—

Patience: Q. What is a whalebone?

Sophie (boredly): A. A sort of gristle found inside the body of a whale which supplies the place of teeth.

Patience: Q. How many are there in each whale?

Sophie (impatiently): A. Four or five hundred.

Patience: Q. What is a whalebone used for?

Sophie: A. To stiffen bodices and umbrellas.

Patience: Q. Are not umbrellas of great antiquity?

Sophie: A. Yes. Greeks and Romans used them to keep off the sun. Ombrello means 'shade' in Italian.

'A little shade,' corrected Patience equably.

It is obvious from the foregoing that Sophie should have breathed a sigh of relief as the first houses of the village came into view. She could, of course, have refused to take part in the senseless catechism, but the questions did serve to pass the time spent in such dull company as Patience had become since her betrothal. Sad but inescapable was the fact that her cousin was no fun at all now that she had grown an invisible outer shell which made her blissfully impervious to slights and taunts.

Mr Smith's spouse, a rotund, exquisitely neat personage, came forward to greet her customers and immediately focused her undivided attention upon Miss Darker, who, having no particular purchase in mind, wasted a great deal of that lady's overdone servility upon the selection of a pair of silk stockings, changing her mind several times before at last rejecting every single pair presented for her inspection.

Patience sat upon a stool and lived up to her name, awaiting her turn as the person of least consequence in the Darker household. She was at last served, and bought a beaded reticule which was far too expensive, simply because she could not bear to put the now perspiring Mrs Smith to any more trouble. The reticule was passed to an assistant to be wrapped in its distinctive pink paper. Sophie meanwhile drew her cousin's attention to a display of embroidered gloves which, according to the label, written in Mr Smith's beautiful copperplate, were the kind previously used by the late lamented Queen of France. This claim produced a sniff of disdain from Sophie. 'How unbusinesslike of Mr Smith not to say that the gloves are as worn by Madame du Barry. They say she is to become the official mistress of King Louis now that the Pompadour is dead.'

Patience made a little noise of sympathy. 'Poor queen, never to have commanded the affection of her husband.'

Sophie gave a careless shrug. 'They say she was much prouder than our Queen, and would never condescend to speak with the common people.'

'Haughtiness is often a convenient mask to conceal the fact that one's pride is hurt,' murmured Patience, and having picked up her neatly-wrapped parcel, bade Mrs Smith a courteous 'Good afternoon, ma'am.'

The two young women had not proceeded a hundred yards up the street, however, when a voice hailing them from behind made them take pause. Turning, they looked back in the direction from when they had come. 'Stop!' Mrs Smith, her round cheeks trembling with indignation, came puffing up, and pointing dramatically to Patience's parcel, which dangled by its string from her wrist, declared in a voice filled with outraged horror, 'Thief!'

Patience went very pale, and her hand shot out in startled denial of the astonishing accusation. Sophie stood rooted to the spot, staring by turns at the parcel and at her cousin. It was Patience who found her voice first. 'Wh...what can you mean, ma'am?'

Mrs Smith, her front of red curls bobbing about frantically under her lace cap, was made almost inarticulate with emotion. 'I m-must...please to step back into the shop, Miss Pochin.'

Patience took refuge in anger. 'Am I to understand, Mrs Smith, that you are accusing me of taking something which does not belong...that is to say, for which I have not paid?'

Mrs Smith nodded emphatically, and stabbing at the parcel again with her forefinger said confidently, 'There is a pair of gloves in your package which does not belong to you.'

'The ones we were looking at?' put in Sophie helpfully.

Mrs Smith accorded her a sharp look but did not presume to question one of the gentry. She reiterated her former request. 'Please, Miss Pochin, will you be good enough to step back into the shop?'

'You have called me a thief, ma'am,' said Patience, low-voiced. Her colour mounted, and the slight unsteadiness of her voice betrayed a nervous anxiety. 'You have yet to prove the charge!'

After flinging down this challenge, she jostled Mrs Smith aside, and with her head held high walked back towards the Emporium.

The parcel, upon being opened, was seen to contain a silver reticule and a pair of embroidered gloves 'as worn by Queen Maria Lesczinska'. Once again the colour fled from Patience's face. 'I did not take them,' she whispered. 'Your assistant must have put them there by mistake.'

The girl assistant, on being questioned, stoutly maintained that the two items had been together on the pink wrapping paper when she came to make up the parcel. 'You put the gloves on top of the reticule when my back was turned,' accused Mrs Smith with increased belligerence.

'No, no, I swear I did not!' Patience, thoroughly rattled now, having become the focal point of interest for several curious customers in the Emporium, burst into tears of fright and bewilderment. Despite her protestations, however, and her appeals to Sophie to bear witness that she had not indulged in any criminal activities, the constable was sent for, and within the space of half an hour Miss Patience Pochin was taken up and held prisoner in the village gaol, there to await transportation to Lewes gaol, where she would languish until the next assizes were held. To the weeping Patience it was like a horrible nightmare. Everything had happened so swiftly, and now her hopes for the future were like charred ashes in her mouth, her heart a black lump of despair.

Clarissa had been jumpy all day, still

upset by the recent death of Tolko, one of the black slaves, and incensed by William's decision to have the man buried in the unconsecrated ground of the garden which surrounded the mausoleum, instead of within the precincts of the parish churchyard. William, unrepentant, had met her protests with cold indifference, and when she had become over-insistent, had snapped at her, 'For God's sake, Clarissa, where the devil did you expect me to bury an unbaptized heathen?'

She had won a weak kind of victory by obtaining her husband's consent to have the rest of the slaves, including Salome, converted to Christianity by the parson, but she was wretchedly conscious of a growing coolness between herself and William, and with irrational perverseness determined that she would wait for him to make the first overtures for peace between them. She was in no mood to be conciliatory, therefore, when the shocking news of Patience's arrest was conveyed by a round-eyed, breathless Sophie, who had run all the way back from the village, bursting to disclose the details of the sorry affair.

Ignoring William's objections, Clarissa insisted upon going down to the village gaol at once. 'Poor girl, we cannot abandon her to her fate. We must see if there is anything she lacks. If they are taking her away tomorrow she will require a change of linen and some articles for her toilet.'

Clarissa pulled distractedly at one of her curls. 'Odd's fish, what a to-do. I find it quite impossible to believe that Patience is a thief. I declare, I shall *not* believe it until it is positively *proved.*' She questioned Sophie for the umpteenth time. 'Try to remember, Sophie, all that passed when you were in the Emporium.'

Now that the excitement had died down a little Sophie was unhelpful. She had seen nothing untoward and was as astonished as all of them at the turn of events. 'All I know is,' she declared emphatically, 'that when the parcel was untied the gloves were lying on top of the reticule.'

A worried Clarissa went herself to supervise the packing up of Patience's effects into the wicker hamper which the girl had brought with her to Frinton Park. She came downstairs a quarter of an hour later, ashen-faced and trembling, and holding in her clenched fist her diamond necklace. Mutely, she held it up for William's inspection. He was astounded.

'You necklace,' he said wonderingly. 'I had forgotten all about it and thought you had recovered it long since. Why did you not tell me that it was still missing?'

She bit her lip. 'I thought whoever had taken it might restore it...perhaps become frightened,' she finished lamely.

He frowned. 'Did you ask Patience about it?'

She answered dully, 'Yes. She denied any knowledge of it.'

'By thunder,' he muttered, 'who would have thought it?' And then, torn between anger and pity at his wife's obvious distress, and fearful for the safety of their child, 'Clarissa, you must not get into a taking because a family dependant turns out to be light-fingered. It has happened before, you know, and will again. Jealousy is generally at the back of it. A girl like Patience sees other ladies in the family wearing fine clothes, making good matches...you know what I mean.'

'But Patience...I still cannot believe...'

He took her by the arm, leading her towards a chair. 'Nor can I, come to that. She has been with us for three years, and never a hint of anything amiss before. The allowance I make her is generous enough for a person in her condition, so I can find little enough excuse for her.'

Clarissa shoved the expensive trinket in the pocket of her gown as though she could not bear to look at it. 'We need not say...' she began, and was halted by William's quick frown of dissent.

'We must,' he argued. 'If we do not, we could be charged with withholding vital evidence concerning her character. That is an offence punishable at law.'

'But if we tell what we know, she is sure to be found guilty!'

'Deuce take it, she *is* guilty!'

Clarissa bit her lip. 'What a scandal this will cause in the county. Surely, William, you will do all in your power to avert it?'

'By attempting to pervert the course of justice? No...no, that will not do at all.' As he said these words William shook his head vigorously before adding, 'The scandal will not be so great. There are many in the county who are not aware that Patience is a family connection. They think of her as a servant, a companion for Sophie.'

'Oh, William...' She longed to berate him for such callousness, but feared to do so lest he forbid her to visit Patience.

Instead, she said, 'Poor Dr Westlake. What will he do?'

William sank into a chair beside his wife. 'Break off his betrothal at once, if he has any sense. It will do his career no good at all if he prolongs his attachment to a common felon.'

'William, I beg you not to call her that.' Awakening anger had a bracing effect upon Clarissa's spirits, dispelling the gloomy lethargy which had resulted on the discovery of the necklace. She said firmly, 'I shall begin by going down to the gaol to see that she is pretty comfortable. There is probably some perfectly reasonable explanation as to how the necklace came to be in her room.'

William was cynical. 'It did not fly there, and if she denied any knowledge of it before, how can she explain it away now?'

Clarissa made a fresh attempt to persuade her husband to take a broader view of the situation. 'Must we tell the authorities about the necklace? It is not as if it has any bearing on the other offence.'

William tried to hide his impatience. 'Were Salome and Sophie with you when you found it?'

'Yes, they were helping me with Patience's things.'

'Then you have answered your own question. To expect Sophie to keep silent upon so titillating a matter would be like expecting the sun to rise in the west.'

She returned sharply, 'Sophie could be coerced into silence and Salome has sufficient dignity to remain so.'

William was about to reply when a high voice cut across their exchange. 'If Patience is found guilty at her trial, will she be hanged or transported?' Sophie had come into the morning-room unheard.

Clarissa twisted round in her chair to stare at her sister-in-law incredulously. Both possibilities appalled her. 'She cannot be *hanged* for stealing a pair of gloves!'

Sophie's cat-smile froze Clarissa's blood. 'She can hang for stealing something from a shop, if the value of the said article or articles exceeds the sum of forty shillings...the gloves were marked at two guineas. They were embroidered with gold thread.'

Like a magic-lantern slide, there came flashing upon Clarissa's inner eye an image of Sophie poring over one of William's books in the library, a law book, the sort of weighty treatise which would contain such jargon as 'value of the said article or articles...'

Patience, perched awkwardly on a hard wooden stool, was pale and restrained, clearly doing battle with herself in order to maintain a respectable degree of self-control.

'I have brought one or two necessary articles,' Clarissa said, depositing the hamper on the stone floor. The smallness of the cell oppressed her. It was no bigger than a closet, and the whitewashed walls, while augmenting the meagre pin-points of light filtering through the tiny barred window, created the awful sensation that she had been entombed alive. This impression was heightened by the lowness of the ceiling. Clarissa's gaze travelled upwards almost fearfully, and then was lowered as Patience addressed her.

'That is very kind of you, Cousin Clarissa.' A faint flicker of a smile hovered about the young woman's lips, bravely held there for the fraction of a second before it disappeared behind the tightly closed mouth.

'Are you quite comfortable?' asked

Clarissa, and immediately felt extremely foolish. The irony of the question escaped Patience, however. She was concerned only with the clearing of her good name. The rough-hewn, inanimate stool and wooden bed, the barred window, the obvious bucket, meant nothing at all, since they could not speak in her defence. Only the living, ushered into her cell with a rattle of the gaoler's keys, could help her. She clung to Clarissa's presence as she would to a piece of wood drifting in a boundless ocean. 'I am innocent,' she declared at once. 'Dare I hope that you believe that, Clarissa?'

Clarissa, who could not bear to encounter the anguished gaze of the wide-set brown eyes, compellingly earnest and frank, opened her reticule and drew forth the necklace. Patience looked at it briefly and then up at Clarissa with puzzled curiosity. 'You found it, then? I am so glad. It would have pained you to lose Mr Darker's gift.'

'I came upon it in your room, Patience, in the drawer of your boudoir-table. I discovered it while I was looking for your toilet articles.'

'Oh, but how could that be? I really

do not see...oh, heavens, *that* is why you brought it here!' Patience rose clumsily to her feet, knocking over the stool. 'You cannot think that *I* stole it?'

Clarissa's heart stirred to pity. The impeccably neat Patience, no longer cool and composed, her pale hair straggling out of its smooth plait to harass her flushed cheeks and cling stickily to her forehead, stood before her wringing her hands and begging her to judge here and now, because it was so terribly important that someone should believe in her innocence.

'No, I do not think that you stole it, Patience,' Clarissa said quietly, more to ease the pain in the other's eyes than because she was entirely convinced by her fervent declaration of innocence. 'But others might do so.'

Patience's eyes widened into shocked disbelief. 'Oh, no, they could not possibly think that. I...' She made a desperate appeal. 'Shall you help me?'

'To the very best of my ability. I shall certainly speak in your defence in regard to the necklace.' And that is about all I can do for you, Clarissa said to herself, unless... She left the train of thought unpursued, and by dint of comforting words and gentle persuasion coaxed the story of the afternoon's adventure from the unhappy prisoner. Nothing significant emerged to contradict the story told by Sophie, and Clarissa left the gaol with a heavy weight of doubt oppressing her spirit.

16

The Countess Is Laid To Rest And Richard Darker Is Married

The little Countess was laid to rest in the Darker family mausoleum pending instructions from France, and a priest was summoned from Brighthelmstone to say the burial service over her.

'I cannot go down there,' Clarissa told William. 'It might harm the baby.'

'Nonsense,' he retorted. 'Our mausoleum is not a place to fear. I have had it decorated inside with Italian mosaic-work. It is really quite beautiful. There is nothing to see, if that is what you are afraid of. The coffins are placed in the vaults below a year after death.'

Her troubled face lost its anxious frown.

'No,' he said, understanding well her fear, 'Frances is not there now.'

His forthright, calm manner made her feel ashamed. 'You must not be afraid of death, Clarissa. It comes to all of us sooner or later.'

She smiled and nodded her head. 'A woman with child is a poor, vulnerable creature, William. She is full of foolish imaginings.'

'Foolish, indeed,' he agreed with a smile. 'You are a fine, healthy girl, Clarissa. You will give me a child and survive to nurse it.'

It was a sad little procession that made its way to the mausoleum. The whole family was present, William going first through the opened wrought-iron gates, and leading the way along the brick path which terminated in a wide flight of steps. Up the steps they went, under the line of Doric columns, and on to the carved oaken door. Clarissa, stepping over the threshold, could not hold back a little gasp of astonishment at the splendour of the interior. Patterns in pink, blue and gold mosaic-work lined the walls, and the domed ceiling showed Christ in Majesty presiding over the obsequies of the faithful taking place below. Six stained-glass windows depicting scenes from the Crucifixion let in a great deal more light than was usual in such places.

The priest was kind and understanding, and thanked William for his consideration and tactful handling of such a delicate situation, assuring him that he would perform no rites which could possibly give offence to him or to his family. The full burial service, according to the rites of the Roman Catholic Church, would not be performed until the Countess's body was back in her native land.

After the conclusion of the simple ceremony William took the priest aside. 'If there should be any difficulty about sending the body back to France...' He hesitated briefly, 'What I mean to say is, the lady was the wife of a convicted traitor, and it may very well be that she will have to be interred permanently here in England in order to avoid embarrassment to her relatives abroad.'

The priest, a pale young man who had only recently taken orders, looked grave. 'Would you be agreeable to her body remaining here, sir?'

'Of course. The lady was my cousin.'

'In that case I should be obliged to perform the full rites of our Church.'

'I shall do nothing to prevent it.'

'You are more than generous, sir,'

'People may worship as they please, so far as I am concerned,' returned William gruffly.

A month after the tragedy, Richard Darker, his arm still in a sling, was married to Caroline Aynge at the parish church. Both of Clarissa's sisters were invited to the wedding, but only Georgiana attended, Ann pleading an indisposition which everyone believed in except Clarissa. The day after the wedding, when Richard and Caroline had departed for London to begin their married life together, a wedding-tour having been happily dispensed with by both parties, Clarissa rode over to her old home at Varracombe Hall to see her youngest sister, whom she came upon in the garden, listlessly cutting the dead heads off the rose bushes.

Ann's face showed the marks of tears shed the night long. Soap and water, rigorously applied upon rising, had failed to eradicate them. Clarissa looked gravely at these overt signs of grief. 'Richard Darker was not for you, my dear Ann. He is a man of the world...experienced. He would have broken your heart.'

Ann stared blankly at her sister. 'Am I to understand, Clarissa, that you think me so foolish as to pine for Mr Darker? Let me assure you that I care nothing for him.'

'Is it your custom to weep on behalf of those for whom you do not care?'

Ann denied hotly that she had been weeping. 'My head was so painful yesterday that it has quite spoiled my looks.'

Clarissa, who had been prepared to offer the soothing syrup of kind words and to make proposals for an excursion to Brighthelmstone, in order to sample the delights of sea-dipping, was a little put out by this cool reception of her well-meant overtures. 'I see that you are not yet *quite* recovered,' she said pointedly.

Ann snipped busily away at the roses. 'Have you received word from France about the Countess?'

Clarissa shook her head, relieved that her sister had turned the conversation. 'Not yet. I fear the poor little thing will have to remain in our mausoleum, far from her loved ones.'

'Has Cornelius discovered who informed on him?'

Clarissa frowned. 'Not to my knowledge.'

Ann dropped a dead rose into the trug hooked over her arm. 'Papa is quite put out about Cornelius and Richard. It places him in a very awkward position. As a magistrate he has always condemned the practice of smuggling.'

'Papa shall not be embarrassed,' Clarissa returned quickly. 'William has warned Cornelius that he is to behave himself in future, and that he must find some other outlet for his energies. If the Countess had not died, Papa would never have known about Cornelius's comings and goings between England and France.

'Perhaps it is as well that Papa found out,' Ann said. 'There was always the risk that Cornelius would be caught, and it would have been extremely discommoding for you to have a brother-in-law put up before the assizes.

This remark reminded Clarissa of Patience. 'I fear that I shall have to attend the assizes at Lewes next month when Patience comes up for trial, a most distasteful prospect to look forward to.'

'What a foolish creature she must be,'

said her sister, 'to take the risk of stealing a paltry pair of gloves, just when she is about to be married.'

'I do not believe for one moment that she did steal them,' Clarissa repeated for the thousandth time.

'Then how, pray, did the gloves get into the parcel she took from the Emporium?'

Clarissa sighed and shook her head. 'I do not know. It is so completely out of character for Patience to do a thing like that.'

'Perhaps she grew tired of living on charity and of always having to purchase articles of inferior quality,' Ann said. 'Did she not have a father in humble circumstances and a horde of younger brothers and sisters?'

'Yes. According to William, she sent them money every month.'

'Sophie says that she stole one of your necklaces, too.'

'Sophie should learn to keep a still tongue in her head,' Clarissa snapped back crossly.

'Did she?' Ann persisted.

'I do not know. Certainly my necklace was missing, and certainly it was found in Patience's room, but I am sure that there was some mistake. She did not mean to keep it.'

'Is she to be accused of taking the necklace?'

'Yes...no! Oh, I do not know!' Clarissa put a hand to her forehead. 'Really, your manners leave much to be desired, Ann. You are too inquisitive by half.'

As Clarissa drove the gig home she could not shake off the restless irritability which the interview with her sister had engendered. The unfortunate affair of Patience Pochin had been nagging at the back of her mind for days. Why was William so insistent that charges for stealing the necklace must be laid with the justices against Patience, when he knew that she might suffer a far more severe penalty if the case were proved, than she would for the stealing of a pair of gloves? Despite Sophie's glib quoting of the law, Clarissa was convinced that a word from William in the right quarter could stave off a capital sentence. As for the matter of the necklace, that could easily be hushed up and kept within the family circle—servants could be threatened with dismissal and Sophie with any number of dire consequences—but William must needs go chasing off to Lewes especially to lay further charges against his wretched cousin as though, poor thing, she were not in enough trouble already. It was almost as if...but Clarissa would not give credence to the thoughts which kept insinuating their way into her head. Thank heaven when the trial was over. At least the worst would be known.

17

Patience Pochin Is Put Upon Her Trial

The gaol for the large and populous town of Lewes was called the Dungeon. It consisted of a haphazard collection of grey stone buildings enclosing a courtyard some twenty-five feet square, in which as many as two hundred prisoners, male and female, were 'exercised' daily. Cells, two in number, were provided to accommodate the inmates. These foetid holes were situated under the gaoler's house, access to them being gained by the descent of seven stone steps, treacherous with slime and the excrement of the gaoler's dog. Bedding for the prisoners was made up of wooden boards upon which a meagre quantity of straw was laid, the latter being renewed twice a year.

In these unsalubrious apartments persons of both sexes were herded together during the day-time, decency being observed by the removal of the women in the evening to two night-rooms on the opposite side of the court. As dusk fell each evening, a procession of bedraggled creatures would make its way across the courtyard, skirting the stagnant puddle in which the gaoler's ducks splashed miserably around, awaiting their summons to the kitchen-block, and enter the 8' x 5' cells which would accommodate them until the coming of dawn, and from when they would issue, unrested and heavy-eyed, to face another interminable day.

Patience found these nightly incarcerations almost beyond her capacity to endure, and passed the hours of darkness crouched in a corner of one of the cells with her knees hunched up to her chin. A whole week went by before anyone ventured to approach her, her ladylike appearance making her an immediate object of suspicion.

Pretty Hayes, in again for vagrancy, and facing a sentence of seven years' transportation to Botany Bay, was the first to overcome her 'scruples'.

'What you in for, dearie?' Pretty sidled closer to the huddled figure in the corner which instinctively recoiled at the odour she exuded. 'Not murder, is it?' The suggestion seemed to amuse Pretty. She cackled loudly and explored her greasy hair with one long fingernail.

'No,' replied Patience faintly. Rising to her feet, she shrank back against the damp stone wall of the female felons' quarters as though she would press herself through it.

Pretty eyed her up and down, expertly assessing the quality of her attire, and deciding that the onyx brooch pinned to the lady's bodice was worth a go at the famble's cheat.

A thin, dirty child came up and clawed at Patience's skirt. Pretty clouted the lice-infested head with her clenched fist, and the child ran off, holding her ear and whining. An extraordinarily swift rush of colour flooded Patience's cheeks as she remonstrated, 'Really, there was no need to do that.'

'She's my kid,' Pretty retorted belligerently. 'I do as I like wiv 'er.'

Patience, who was in no condition to fight the good fight, subsided into miserable silence.

'What you done then, to get put in 'ere?' the obstinate creature demanded again.

'I have done nothing.' Patience tried to sound dignified.

Pretty laughed again, an awful noise which turned into a series of racking coughs. 'That's what they all say, dearie.'

'It is true,' came the cold affirmation, and then, because the tears were beginning to prick at the back of her eyelids, and because even to talk to this horrid, depraved woman was better than talking to oneself, Patience said, 'I am accused of stealing a pair of gloves from a shop.' She went on to recount the circumstances surrounding her arrest, telling of her consternation when Mrs Darker had mentioned the missing necklace. By the time she had finished her recital Pretty was eyeing her with great speculation, her small brown eyes screwed up tight.

'Oh, my dearie,' she said, 'looks to me like you been framed. I can tell a liar when I sees one, and you ain't a liar, that's for sure.' She shrugged her thin shoulders, intrigued by the tale, yet too lethargic to pursue its intricacies further. 'Better get yourself a good lawyer, m'dear,' she advised, '''cos 'ooever's got it in for you is doing a right good job of bringin' you down.'

Mr Braithwaite faced the prisoner across the hard wooden table, observing her hand manacles with indignant distaste. 'I shall get those removed before this day is out,' he promised, and received in return a wan smile of gratitude. The lawyer coughed to hide his embarrassment, and brought forth a sheaf of papers from the leather portfolio which he had placed on the table between himself and his client. 'As I think you know, Miss Pochin, I am Mr Darker's attorney-at-law. I have been retained by the said gentleman in this case to defend you, and I am sure that I need not assure you that I shall do everything that lies in my power to help you.'

'Mr Darker is very kind.' As she said these words, something began to nag at the back of Patience Pochin's brain, a memory from a good while ago which tantalisingly eluded capture. The memory was so faint that, weighed down as she was by a feeling of deep depression, Patience quickly gave up the struggle to bring it to light and endeavoured to give her full attention to Mr Braithwaite, who was asking her to recall the details of her shopping expedition. 'Every smallest detail you can remember, Miss Pochin,' he insisted.

Sighing, she went over the whole thing again, as she had done a thousand times in her own mind. While she was speaking he nodded several times, busily squeaking away with a charcoal stick on the piece of paper which lay before him. 'And the necklace?' he inquired with studied casualness. He did not look up.

'I know nothing of the necklace.'

At this his head was raised and a deeply penetrating glance was directed at her. 'But surely, Miss Pochin, you must know something. The necklace did not walk of its own accord into your bedroom.'

Woodenly, she repeated her denial. 'I have not the least idea how the necklace came to be in my room.'

Neither by dint of persuasion, nor by outright hints that she might find herself in even graver trouble, could the lawyer move Patience to speak of the necklace. Inwardly, he confessed that the outlook was gloomy for Miss Pochin. 'Touching the matter of the gloves,' he said aloud, 'it is possible that we may get over it by pleading absent-mindedness on your part...your approaching nuptials...much on your mind. It is not inconceivable that you might have inadvertently picked up the gloves and put them on top of the other article which you had lawfully purchased.'

Her eyes held the chill of despair. 'Unless my mind is deranged, Mr Braithwaite, there is no way I could have put those gloves into the parcel without remembering that I had done so.' She added for good measure, 'I do not think that I am mad.'

'But Miss Pochin,' he said rather desperately, 'you would be prepared to state in court, would you not, that this is how it *might* have happened? You would be prepared to concede that you might just possibly have...?'

She cut swiftly across these worried meanderings. 'I shall not perjure myself in court, Mr Braithwaite, especially since I shall be required to place my hand upon a Holy Bible and swear to tell the exact truth.'

Head-shakings accompanied his brief sigh of exasperation. God protect him from stubborn and pious women. 'Then I cannot guarantee that a verdict of Not Guilty will be returned,' he warned, looking at her over the top of his square-framed spectacles.

The threat of transportation or worse did not appear to alarm her. She said calmly, 'I must rely upon the truth and upon my innocence to protect me, Mr Braithwaite.'

'I pray God that it will,' he returned drily.

That night, over his glass of port and lemon, Mr Braithwaite confided to his wife the fact the he very much feared Miss Pochin would shortly find herself upon a ship bound for Botany Bay unless she could be brought to see sense. Being a kindly man, the lawyer refused to consider that other, more awful alternative.

'I do not think it advisable for you to go to such a place in your delicate condition. We can wait in the "White Hart", and if she is found guilty on the first charge of stealing the gloves we shall not be required to give evidence on the second charge concerning the necklace. The second charge will be dropped,' he emphasised. 'I have seen to that. Sophie will have to go, of course. She is to give evidence.'

William's voice seemed unnaturally loud to Clarissa. He is speaking to me as though I am a deaf old lady, she thought with a touch of annoyance. She did not allow her irritation to show, for she knew from experience that when one wanted a favour it was best to adopt a conciliatory attitude.

'Please, William,' she pleaded, laying a timid hand on his arm. 'Patience has no one except us to befriend her. She begged me not to tell her father of the trouble she is in, and much against my better judgement I forbore to write to him.'

A flicker of indecision in her husband's eyes encouraged her to go on. 'Imagine how it will be for her, William, entering the courtroom with all those staring faces directed towards her. If I am there, at least a smile, if not a word, can be exchanged. I only have to sit down. There will be no undue exertion involved.'

'What if she is found guilty and the judge sentences her to be transported? Will not the shock be too much for you?'

Her chin lifted. 'I am prepared for that, and should be ashamed to play the coward's part, skulking at home while she whom I genuinely like and respect suffers such a dreadful ordeal quite alone.'

Her words seemed to have their effect. He nodded, if a trifle reluctantly, and said, 'I shall drive you and Sophie to Lewes myself and wait for you at the inn. My presence in the court-room would, I feel, only cause distress to Patience, since she knows that through me she could be charged with the theft of your necklace.'

Clarissa seized this opportunity to make a further request. 'Is it too late to drop the charge concerning the necklace? Altogether, I mean...whatever happens?'

He frowned. 'Not too late, my dear, but injudicious. I have my position in the county to consider. If it ever got out that I shielded a criminal I should stand little chance of taking over your father's seat in Parliament when he retires.'

His tone told her that the subject was closed, and she dared not pursue it further in case he went back on his promise to allow her to attend the trial. Abruptly, he changed the subject. 'Someone has left a dead cockerel in the garden of the mausoleum. Its head is half-severed and there's a mess of blood on the steps. You have not observed anyone hanging around there, I suppose?'

She shook her head, looking puzzled. 'Who could have done it?'

'I do not know.' William sounded vaguely annoyed. 'It is not one of our birds, so I am inclined to suspect a thief taking the short cut through my property at night. Perhaps he was pursued and dumped the bird in case he was caught.'

'How very strange,' murmured Clarissa.

On the second day of the assizes, when four cases were to be tried before Mr Justice Brockley of Findon Valley, the town of Lewes seethed with people, the majority of whom frankly hoped to see a hanging. Not many assizes went by without resulting in at least one such dubious spectacle, and the gallows was always set up outside the courthouse ready to receive Mr Justice Brockley's offerings, and also to inspire in those who escaped with their lives a proper humility and a powerful incentive not to do wrong in the future. The word among the crowd was that at least one hanging could be looked for come Thursday, because on that day a man was to be tried for doing away with his wife. In the case of females, married or unmarried, there would be a four-week delay 'to determine whether or not the prisoner's belly be great'.

Clarissa, leaning heavily on William's arm, and with Sophie lagging behind, gave a little shudder as she caught sight of the grisly instrument and hurried past it, dragging her husband through the milling throng. The courthouse was on the north side of the market square, and already a number of people were converging on the double doors which were presently opened wide.

Mounting the steps, they were met by an usher who inquired as to the nature of their business. After a brief whispered consultation with William, the usher undertook to see that the ladies were looked after. A shilling discreetly changed hands, after which William retired to the adjacent hostelry, there to linger until the dinner hour, by which time judgement upon Patience should surely have been delivered.

The smell of oranges in the courtroom made Clarissa's stomach heave, but she was determined not to let Patience down. Come what may, she would remain where she was until the prisoner's fate was decided upon. The usher worked well for his silver piece. He guided Clarissa and Sophie to a place in the second row of the witnesses' benches and provided them with grubby velveteen cushions to put behind their backs. Clarissa thanked him with a smile and looked about her. The courtroom was filling rapidly now. She caught sight of Mr Braithwaite, wig askew, consulting with his Clerk, and the nervousness which clutched at her throat and stomach began to abate a little. Mr Braithwaite had always, by his brisk and forthright manner, inspired her with confidence in his legalistic abilities, though he had never before been called upon to assist the family on a matter of a criminal nature. As well as being William's lawyer, Mr Braithwaite also worked for Clarissa's father, and he it was who had drawn up her marriage contract. A solid, dependable sort of man was Mr Braithwaite. Patience could not be in safer hands.

Clarissa's eyes sought out prosecuting counsel, and were rewarded by the sight of a tall, beak-nosed individual who continually coughed behind his hand, fluttering his long white fingers the while with womanish delicacy. He was making a great to-do with his papers and firing off a series of asides at Mr Braithwaite. That gentleman seemed to think these broadsides highly amusing, and the two laughed together quite heartily, prosecuting counsel displaying a number of large and patently false china teeth. Clarissa could form no opinion of the prosecuting gentleman. He might or might not be dangerous.

She glanced at Sophie, who was unusually quiet. Lips pursed, her thin face devoid of expression, Sophie stared about her abstractedly, her thoughts contained and private. Clarissa ventured no remark lest the unpredictable girl say something which would set her nerves a-flutter again.

The first shock Clarissa received that day was when Patience was brought up from the bowels of the earth below the courthouse, her arm firmly grasped by a dragon-like female garbed in black, whose grey hair was screwed into a tight knot on the top of her head. The waist of the dragon lady was encircled by a metal chain, from which grim ornament hung a formidable assortment of keys. The keys gave out little metallic clicks as she moved.

This unprepossessing personage pushed

Patience into a cage-like contraption which she locked after her, and then stood back, arms rigidly at her sides, but ready, one surmised, to spring into action if the prisoner should suddenly make an unexpected move. The woman never took her eyes off her charge, the lightless blue orbs seeming to be irremovably attached to the prisoner's back, and imbued with the holding power of a limpet. How pale Patience is, thought Clarissa, and how very thin she has become. She looks at least ten years older than when I saw her last, and her eyes are enormous. Heavens, she is scared to death!

By sitting up a little straighter and leaning forward on the bench Clarissa made every effort to catch Patience's eye, in order that she might smile at her reassuringly, thus conveying the comfortable knowledge that there was a friend close at hand. Patience, however, seemed oblivious of her surroundingss. She looked neither to the right nor to the left, but stared straight in front of her with those dreadfully terror-stricken eyes. Clarissa slowly relaxed back into her seat. She would try again later after the proceedings had commenced.

For the next three hours the two women listened, one with ever increasing despair, to the weight of evidence brought by the prosecution against the prisoner. Several witnesses who said they had been present in the shop at the time of the alleged theft came forward to bear testimony that they had seen the prisoner 'acting strange-like and furtive'. Not one would actually say, however, that he or she had seen the prisoner take the gloves, though the judge, to Clarissa's amazement, appeared very much inclined to accept opinion and hearsay as solid fact.

Sophie's evidence neither helped nor hindered Patience's chances of acquittal. She had been there, but she had seen nothing. Mr Braithwaite pressed her hard, but she remained adamant that she had been looking at some parasols at the far end of the Emporium from where her cousin was making her purchases.

In his summing-up, Mr Braithwaite made great play over Miss Pochin's respectability, while prosecuting counsel in *his* summing-up made great play over Miss Pochin's undeniably penurious condition. Mr Justice Brockley came suspiciously near to nodding off during counsels' concluding arguments. Having already made up his own mind that the prisoner was guilty as sin, he drifted off into a fascinating reverie in which he knelt before the King and swore allegiance as His Majesty's Lord Chancellor. Mr Justice Brockley could almost feel the soft texture of the royal skin against his as His Majesty offered his hand to be kissed. 'I shall seek your advice upon every matter appertaining to the laws of the realm,' promised King George...

An expectant hush in the courtroom brought Mr Justice Brockley back to harsh reality with a start. After a moment's hesitation, during which the red face of the King faded sadly away, he briefly directed his blank-faced jury to find the prisoner guilty, which, to Clarissa's dismay, they did, without even bothering to retire.

While he waited for the jury's decision, Mr Justice Brockley's stomach began to rumble. He thought of the dinner of pork chops, green beans and a mountain of potatoes promised by the landlord of the 'White Hart'. The doleful emptiness of his belly made Mr Justice Brockley a thought spiteful. It was his considered opinion that these female shop thieves should be made an example of.

Patience Pochin stood listening impassively while sentence of death was passed upon her—the said sentence to be carried out after the expiration of four weeks, 'by which time it will be apparent whether or no the prisoner's belly be great'.

Amid the rising hum of speculation Clarissa, despite her previous fervent assurances to the contrary, fainted clean away.

18

New Evidence

Salome squeezed her thin body through the broken palings, the bleeding cockerel clutched tightly in her hand. Peering anxiously to right and left, for she was very fearful of being observed, she bent double and snaked her way to the steps of the mausoleum. Mounting swiftly, she deposited the cockerel on the top step, and dabbling her fingertips in the ooze of blood from the bird's neck, smeared a crude representation of a male figure beside the inanimate mound of feathers. To the uninitiated eye, Salome's handiwork was indistinguishable from the messy little puddle of gore resultant upon the placing of the dead bird on the steps. Not until she was completely satisfied that the correct signs had been made, however, did she draw back and descend the steps.

She was about to move swiftly towards her point of ingress when she felt herself being seized from behind by a pair of strong masculine arms and pushed to the ground with the aid of a boot-heel ground into the small of her back. She was too winded to scream, but with the quick instinct of an animal, twisted over on to her back in order to see the face of her attacker.

She gave a little gasp of shock and covered her mouth with her hand, looking up at the man who had surprised her, with her great staring eyes exposing whites like polished marble. He straddled her body with his booted feet and, leaning down, dug his fingers into her woolly hair. Obtaining a firm hold, he gave her head a hard, painful jerk. 'What are you doing here?'

She stifled a shriek as his other hand

was raised to strike her if she made a sound. 'Sir!' she babbled. 'I ain't done no harm, sir!' I just done brung a sacrifice for the lady.'

He gave her head another savage jerk. 'Why?'

Her mouth opened and shut as she sought desperately to find an answer that would please him, and satisfy him that she was working no evil. If he knew the truth he would kill her. She had seen and overheard something which had brought all the old superstitious fears of her native land bubbling to the surface, a horde of black devils which must be appeased if trouble was not to come to the house. Was it not written in the laws of her tribe that if a man or woman met death by an act of violence, evil spirits would haunt those who had brought it about unless offerings were made? As it was, she was not doing it right. Human sacrifice was what was needed, but what a terrible to-do there would be if she left a dead child at the door of this Christian burial place. A cockerel's blood could be smeared in the correct voodoo pattern to quieten the devils, but its magic was not as powerful as the blood of a child.

She had done the best she could for her countryman amongst these unbelievers. For an instant her eyes flickered towards the mound of freshly-turned earth near the gates. They had put Tolko as far away from their own gods as they could, she thought with vindictive hatred, then, fearing that the boss-man might read something from her expression and guess her secret, she whispered, 'The poor lady, sir. No one done brung her a sacrifice 'cept me.'

'Lying bitch!' He shook her head from side to side as it if had been a freshly uprooted cabbage. 'D'ye think I don't know your heathenish voodoo when I see it? I knew it was you as soon as I saw that first cockerel. Appeasing the gods, are you? What for? What for?'

Tears ran down her black cheeks on to the brutally clenched hand which hovered dangerously near her mouth. 'Sir, please, sir, don't kill me!'

He was not quite sure what she had seen or heard, but he was certain that his power over her was such that she would never dare to open her mouth for fear he might kill her. As to that, he had not quite made up his mind. 'Keep your black mouth shut, d'ye hear?'

She nodded, frantically gulping back the sobs that threatened to choke her. With a single swift movement of his arm, he hoisted her to her feet. 'Meet me down at the cove after dark tonight,' he instructed, 'and liven yourself up a bit. I don't want to pleasure myself on a piece of dead mutton.'

The woman sat facing Clarissa, twisting the strings of her blue serge cloak in nervous, work-roughened hand. 'I would not have come,' she admitted, directing a troubled glance at this elegantly gowned lady who was big with child, 'but when I heard that the lady was to be hanged, I said to my husband that I must speak out, or go to my grave with a terrible weight of sin upon my conscience.'

Clarissa, in whose breast a small spark of hope had been ignited, leaned forward, and with an imploring gesture of her hand said earnestly, 'Please, Mrs Clayton, if you have anything to tell me concerning Miss Pochin, you will do me the greatest possible service.'

The woman shifted uneasily on the sofa, as though unaccustomed to taking her ease upon so fine a piece of furniture. 'I was there, ma'am, in the Emporium, when the lady and her friend came in.'

'My sister-in-law, Miss Sophie Darker, was with Miss Pochin,' put in Clarissa.

Mrs Clayton nodded impatiently, plainly indicating that exact relationships were of very little consequence to her. 'I was buying some of that new coffee-coloured lace for my mistress, Lady Villeneau of Blandon Hall, and I saw Mr Smith come through from the back of the Emporium and put that pair of gloves...green, they were, worked with gold thread...in the lady's parcel when she had turned aside to look at something else.' She shook her head in bewilderment. 'Don't ask me why he did it, ma'am. I didn't think much of it at the time. I thought p'rpaps the lady had ordered the gloves, and that Mr Smith had put them by for her. Later, I came to remember how he was there one minute and gone like a flash the next. Queer it was.' She shook her head again. ''Tis a mystery to me, unless 'twas done to get the lady into trouble on purpose like. When I told my husband about it, he said it was best not to meddle.'

Clarissa could not help feeling angry at the nature of this confession. Being an imaginative person herself, she could well understand Patience's present state of mind, and, in truth, having seen her in the courtroom at Lewes, with her dull, listless demeanour and staring, vacant eyes, she had begun to fear for her reason. It was not fifteen days since the trial and there was not very much time left. Enough, thank God, to present this new and startling piece of evidence to the justices. What Mrs Clayton had revealed puzzled Clarissa not a little. She could not have invented such a tale...Why should she?...And yet...

With deliberate intent to provoke a reaction, she voiced her doubts. 'You are quite sure, are you not, Mrs Clayton, that what you have told me is the exact truth?'

The affronted expression in the other woman's eyes would have amused Clarissa in other circumstances. As it was, she had felt compelled to ask the question, since Patience's life might depend upon the answer.

Mrs Clayton sat up very straight and started to replace her discarded gloves. 'My eyes are as good as the next person's, ma'am, and if you'll forgive me saying so, I know what I saw, and what I saw I have revealed to you.'

'Yes...thank you. Indeed, I am most grateful to you, Mrs Clayton,' Clarissa said. 'The matter shall be investigated at once. You may rest easy on that.'

She rose to her feet, her visitor immediately following suit. 'I hope, ma'am,' began Mrs Clayton, and hesitated clumsily while a slow flush mounted her cheeks. 'I mean to say, I hope there will be no trouble coming to me and my man...' Her voice tailed off.

Now that her first anger had passed, Clarissa felt rather sorry for the woman. No doubt Mrs Clayton had thought that Patience would be rescued by her wealthy protectors. Such things happened quite frequently. Come to think of it, whispered a voice in her ear, why had not a 'miracle' happened on this occasion? A bribe to the magistrates, a word or two in the right ear would not be beyond William Darker's power to accomplish.

'You may be required to give evidence,' Clarissa said aloud, 'but I do not see how anyone can reproach you for a temporary loss of memory. No doubt you had many things on your mind that day.'

Mrs Clayton's worried eyes lit up as she grabbed the lifeline thrown out to her.

'Oh, yes, ma'am, I did. Lady Villeneau wanted me to purchase embroidery silks and ribbons, *and* shoe buckles, and I was run off my feet.'

Having helped Mrs Clayton to salve her conscience, Clarissa manoeuvred her gently towards the door and into the waiting hands of the parlour-maid who showed her out. Then she sat down to think.

The first question that inevitably presented itself to her distracted mind was why had Mr Smith put the gloves into the parcel? The sole conclusion to be drawn was that the gentleman in question must have been paid handsomely to do so, in order that Patience would be taken up as a thief. Who would want Patience to get into such serious trouble that it might well cost her her life? Sophie? Sophie had been jealous of Patience ever since her cousin's betrothal to Dr Westlake had been announced. Sophie was a vengeful creature, though Clarissa found it difficult to accept the fact that she would go to the length of allowing another woman to be hanged for something she had not done.

Clarissa's head started to ache at the same time as the baby jumped inside her and set up a little flurry which made her feel sick. She put one hand to her head and the other to her distended abdomen. William would have to deal with this latest development. She would tell him about it immediately he came in.

William was frankly incredulous. 'Mrs Clayton, did you say? Is she an honest sort of person?'

'I am sure that she is.' Clarissa sounded agitated. 'William, please, you will tell the justices about this new evidence? We must do everything in our power to help Patience.'

William fingered his lip with an air of great deliberation. 'Mmm. I wonder whether it is worth it? It seems to me that this Mrs Clayton of yours is simply filled with a desire to be noticed. It is a very common affliction among the working classes.'

'No!' Clarissa wrung her hands. 'I am quite certain that she was speaking the truth.'

His shoulders heaved in a sigh of exasperation as he admonished, 'You must not distress yourself so, Clarissa. God be thanked when the whole miserable business is over and done with.'

'When Patience is hanged and in her coffin, you mean.'

He regarded her curiously, his eyes betraying the faintest hint of hostility. 'She is a thief, you know.'

'No, I do not know!' exclaimed his wife, her voice soaring. 'I shall never believe that she took those gloves.'

'Rather would you believe that Mr Smith, for some purpose known only to God and himself, foisted the gloves upon her?'

'Sophie!' she blurted.

He frowned. 'What of Sophie?'

His manner alarmed her. She had never seen him so edgy, but the growing suspicion that her sister-in-law was in some way involved in the strange affair of the gloves prompted her to speak out. 'It is my opinion that Sophie may have bribed Mr Smith to put the gloves in the parcel. She was jealous because Patience was to marry Dr Westlake. You cannot deny that Sophie has harboured a childish passion for the physician ever since he came to this household.'

William made an explosive sound of disgust and thrust his hands on his hips under his frock-coat. 'That was over long ago.'

'No, William,' she argued, 'it was not. You simply chose to think it was.'

He said nothing for a moment or two, then at length, slapping his thigh, 'I shall speak to Sophie myself, and if she has been up to mischief I shall smoke it out. As to the other matter, I give you my promise that I shall think about it. No!...' The exclamation was drawn from him as she started to protest. 'You have my final word. I shall *think* about it.'

For the next few days she watched him like a cat, but he gave no sign, either that he had spoken to Sophie, or that he had reported Mrs Clayton's confession in the proper quarter. Clarissa, feeling clumsy, and horribly vulnerable in her advanced state of pregnancy, could only wait and pray that all might yet be well. She felt as if she was living through some kind of waking nightmare. Everyone in the household was behaving so very normally. William. Cornelius. Sophie. They all chattered away in the eating-room as though nothing in the world was wrong—worst of all, as though Patience Pochin had never even existed—and as though, when each bright summer morning dawned, the sands of her life would run on for ever.

Clarissa toyed with the idea of writing to Richard, who was still in London, and then had misgivings when she thought of William's reaction if she did anything behind his back. Three days before Patience was due to hang, however, she could stand the suspense no longer. As William prepared to go out on his daily rounds of the estate, she barred his way in the hall. 'What about Patience, William?'

'What *about* Patience?' he repeated provokingly.

'Did you convey Mrs Clayton's information to the justices?'

'I did.'

Tears, which were never very far away these days, sprang to her eyes. 'What did they say?'

'They were not convinced. They shared my opinion that the Clayton woman wants to draw attention to herself.'

'But that is not true! Oh, heavens, I must do something!' Clarissa stared at her husband wildly. 'I must go to Findon and see Mr Justice Brockley myself. Perhaps he will believe me.'

'You will remain here,' he said stonily, 'until after the hanging has taken place.'

Her chin lifted defiantly. 'Do I take you to mean, sir, that I am forbidden to leave the house?'

'I do mean that,' he confirmed with unbending severity, 'and if my orders are disobeyed, you will be pursued, brought back and confined to your room.'

'William,' she pleaded, 'you have always been so kind to me. I do not understand you any longer.'

He reached out, and turning her about, put an arm round her shoulders. 'You must think only of your duty to me, Clarissa. As your husband I have a right to expect that you will give me a child, a living child, whose life you are putting in jeopardy at this very moment by this constant fretting about Patience. What's done is done. It is regrettable, I admit, but Patience should have given heed to what might have been the consequences before she took what did not belong to her.'

Clarissa hung her head and answered, low-voiced, 'I shall never believe that.'

'Believe it or not, the case against Patience has been proved,' he reminded her. 'There was also the matter of the necklace. It was found, by you, in her room.'

'Sophie put it there,' she insisted stubbornly.

He gave her a little shake. 'Sophie is a naughty, mischievous wench, but she is not capable of anything so vile. Give me leave to know the character of my own sister, Clarissa.'

She allowed herself to be comforted, because she did not wish to arouse him yet again to anger, but she was not convinced that everything that was humanly possible had been done to save the life of the miserable girl who lay in the condemned cell of Lewes gaol.

'You done promised to find my man and my children for me, missus.' Salome's large black eyes were accusing as they bored into Clarissa's face.

'And I shall keep that promise, Salome,' Clarissa said gently. 'When my baby is born I shall ask my husband to find out to whom your family were sold, and we shall see if it is possible for you to join them.'

'Master buy me. He no let me go.' Salome did not relax her attitude of fierce hostility.

'Yes, he will,' argued Clarissa. 'He will if I ask him.' She held out her hand to the other. 'I thought you were happy with me, Salome.'

The dark, offended eyes softened a little. 'You been good to me, missus.'

'I said that you would have to wait a little,' she was reminded.

Salome hung her head. 'Yes, missus.'

Clarissa was vaguely puzzled. Salome had seemed so glad to be in a household where she was not ill-treated. For the first few months after William had bought her she had made Clarissa laugh with her tales, sad and bawdy, of life on a sugar plantation. Showing her perfect white teeth in a grin of delight, she would describe the courtship rituals of the young men and women, which sounded so strange to the ears of a white woman, and which were so oddly at variance with anything within Clarissa's range of experience. Her receptive mind was eager for every detail that Salome could remember, and the two would sit for hours, Clarissa with her embroidery, Salome with her mending, talking, talking, talking.

Later, a subtle change had taken place in their relationship. Salome had lost her initial vivacity and frequently lapsed into long silences, during which she would secretly watch Clarissa from beneath absurdly long lashes. Clarissa, conscious of this mute appraisal, which made her feel distinctly uneasy, would try to draw the young woman out, prompting her with such encouragement as 'Tell me again, Salome, about that little boy who put a spider in your hut.' At one time this would have been enough to send Salome off into shrieks of laughter before she settled down to re-tell what had been told a hundred times before. As the weeks went by, however, she responded hardly at all to Clarissa's overtures, hanging her head and saying sullenly, 'I told you, missus, long time ago.'

Clarissa concluded that Salome was pining for her husband and children, and would have asked William to let her go there and then if it had not been for the disaster which had overtaken Patience, and which was pulling her and her husband further and further apart. Persistently tactful questioning had elicited nothing from Salome, and in the end, made apathetic by her pregnancy, Clarissa had given up. She now made up her mind to risk William's displeasure and urge him to let Salome go as soon as possible. Besides, she thought, she reminds me too much of that traffic which I so abhor. She made one last try. 'You are sure that there is nothing troubling you, Salome?'

'No, missus, no trouble.' Again the averted, half-defiant head and the sidelong glance which proclaimed, more loudly than words, that she was lying.

19

Patience Pochin In The Condemned Cell

The erstwhile neat appearance of Patience Pochin had suffered severe ravages during the course of her confinement. She had not washed her hair, nor yet cleaned her teeth for several weeks, and the daily attentions to her hands and face were accomplished with a bowl of dirty water and a fast-disappearing cake of scented soap, the latter thoughtfully provided by Clarissa. Clarissa had also offered to bring in a change of under-linen and a clean dress, but these welcome amenities the prisoner had been forced to decline, since there was nowhere that she could don the articles in question without a hundred eyes peering inquisitively at her and interjecting, for the purposes of general entertainment, comments of a lewd and disgusting nature.

After her trial and condemnation Patience had been taken out of the female felons' quarters and placed in the condemned cell, where it would have been possible to change her clothing in private. This very necessary operation was now denied her by the fact that not a single member of the Darker family, including Clarissa, had bothered to come and see her. The prisoner's growing despair at this cruel neglect was not unmixed with anger. She was no longer of any account in the Darker household, that was clear. They had written her off, as they would write off an old and ailing sheep-dog, except that the dog would have been mercifully shot, while she must endure this hell on earth.

On this day before they were to hang her, Patience sat brooding upon the disasters which had overtaken her, staring the while at her reflection in the piece of broken mirror which lay on the table before her. She remembered an article she had read in the *Ladies' Home Journal* which conveyed to its female readers the interesting information that when one looked down into a mirror one was made instantly aware of a strange phenomenon, to wit, that one's face appeared to be considerably older than when the mirror was propped straight in front of one. '*I* look old from all angles,' Patience said aloud, and picking up the mirror held it closer to her face—'*and* dirty, a verminous female thief, a felon, not fit to live upon this earth with decent people...'

Deliberately, she flayed herself, discovering satisfaction in this mental stoning of a body which she found disgusting and abhorrent. Her eyes had not changed. They were still wide and trusting, certain that the goodness and mercy of God would counteract the cruelty and obscenity of man. There were new lines round her eyes though, lines and dark circles, and there were lines round her mouth, too, and on her forehead. She had aged a hundred years. 'Oh, God, why me?...'

'Why not you?' the mirror mocked her.

She noticed that one of her front teeth was marred by a speck of decay.

The prisoner sat, hands folded meekly on the table before her, listening with polite disinterest to the words of the prison chaplain, who had come to comfort her in her last hours. The long, canting phrases, delivered in the pious monotone thought proper for the saving of a felon's soul, meant less than nothing to her. Patience Pochin, who, for upwards of three years, had dinned into Sophie Darker's unformed mind the tenets of the Protestant faith, by which creed she must endeavour to live her life and strive in the end to obtain entrance to the pearly gates of heaven, could not in turn feel uplifted by one who sought to instruct her and urge her to place her trust in God. Patience Pochin's god had forsaken her. She was convinced that when they perpetrated their act of brutal savagery upon her tomorrow she would descend into a bottomless pit of blackness, a nothingness, a void, from which not even the sound of the last trump could release her. She would be snuffed out like a candle, and her little life would be rounded in a sleep. The words of William Shakespeare, which sprang so readily to her mind, made Patience wish that her copy of the words of the bard was with her now. It would have given her more consolation than the harsh decrees of the Old Testament, which poured off the chaplain's tongue like the milk of human unkindness.

All this for a pair of gloves, a wicked, eight-fingered manifestation which had mysteriously appeared to ruin all her hopes and desires for the future. The small prick of memory which she had experienced in the gaol at Piddingfold, and which had come to her again in the courtroom, when she had spied Clarissa, big with child, sitting on a bench beside Sophie Darker, had now burst forth into the full flower of recognition. It seemed unconnected with her present predicament, and she dismissed it as not worth her consideration. What had happened to the first Mrs Darker could have no bearing upon her present misfortunes or affect her future. Indeed, the word future no longer had any meaning for her. Already the opposite ends of her life were bending towards each other, the superficial trivia of daily existence gradually slipping out of sight, the non-essential paring away, until all that was left was the now, and the few hours of life that remained to her.

At first she had wanted to write to her father to explain that she was not a thief, that there had been some dreadful misunderstanding which time had not resolved, and that she did not want to die leaving him with a bad opinion of her. She had put off writing the letter, and now it was too late, for her drifting mind could never have found the words. A kind of fatalistic euphoria was taking possession of her, like that which overtakes the man who lies freezing in the snow, yet feels warm and comfortable, too comfortable to make the effort to save himself from approaching death.

'Do you truly repent of the sin you have committed?' The chaplain's voice cut across her wandering thoughts. She stared at the round moon face before her, fascinated by the crop of thick curling black hair, and wondered why so young a man had taken over this unenviable job.

She said dully, 'What sin? I have committed no sin, sir.'

He frowned over his prayer-book. 'It is

not good for the soul to meet its Maker unconfessed.'

'Sir,' she replied, 'I cannot confess to something I did not do.'

'So that is the way of it. Stubborn is what you are, Pochin. It is a fault I have discovered to be inherent in every female felon with whom I have come into contact.'

'If by stubbornness, sir, you mean that I refuse to confess to a crime I did not commit,' she retorted hotly, 'then, yes, certainly I am stubborn, and shall continue in that state.'

'You know that you will burn in the fires of hell?'

'No!' She allowed her anger to show. 'I do *not* know that, and nor, sir, do you. God, if there is a God, knows that I am innocent.' Oh, heavens, he was making her aware again, dragging her up from the deep, enclosing well of acceptance, making her conscious of the quick, rhythmic beat of her heart, pounding in time with the prison clock which ticked her life away, making her feel the rapid coming and going of colour in her cheeks, bringing her pulsatingly alive.

'Are you not afraid?' he persisted. She

could not answer him. At this moment she was not afraid, but she very much feared to be afraid on the morrow, when they led her out to die before that gaping crowd. How was it possible, she asked herself, that they could do this thing to her, their fellow human being? But they could. They would. They would lead her out, force her to mount the steps of that horrid wooden contraption in front of a thousand curious eyes. A bag would be put over her head to shut out sight and deaden sound, and then she would feel the harsh hempen noose tighten about her neck... At this point in her musings Patience Pochin turned aside her head and vomited.

When the man of God had departed, with assurances that he would be with her to the last, the raucous tones of the gaoler announced a second visitor. The prisoner looked up with a faint glimmer of hope that her betrothed, whom she had not seen since before her arrest, might have come to offer her one last crumb of comfort.

Cornelius Darker stood in the doorway with a sympathetic look of inquiry upon his face. She rose to her feet as the door clanged to behind him and apologized for the foetid smell permeating the atmosphere, smiling a little as she remembered how fastidious he was.

Cornelius did not appear to notice the very obvious drawbacks to Miss Pochin's lodgings, and after begging her to be seated, propped himself against the wall of the cell. From this point of vantage he regarded her intently, still with that same, faintly inquiring look. She thought: If he asks me how I am I shall scream. But he did not. Instead, he said, 'I have something to tell you, Patience,' and went on to speak for more than half an hour. When he finally took his leave, Patience laid her head upon her folded arms and wept.

20

Clarissa Goes Riding And Is Given An Explanation

On the morning of the day that Patience was to be hanged, Clarissa sat in her bedroom listlessly observing Salome, who was darning a pair of silk stockings. The house seemed very quiet and still. William and Cornelius had ridden to Lewes, presumably to witness the execution, though the exact purpose of their visit had not been specified. Sophie had been despatched to Varracombe Hall to call upon Clarissa's mother and sisters, and only the servants remained. Salome was sunk in her now habitual sullen humour and the door was locked upon them both. Oh, father, thought Clarissa, despairingly, if only you had not gone to London I could have relied on your help, I know.

It seemed to Clarissa that the baby was leaping about inside her with alarming frequency. It frightened her a little, this excess of movement, and the thought of anything happening when she could not move a yard to summon Dr Westlake made her very fearful. She put her fear into words, aiming it at the bowed head of Salome, who instantly looked up and eyed her mistress with some small measure of concern. She does care, thought Clarissa. She has not turned against me, only against the circumstances which bind her to me.

'If you get sick, I climb out window, missus,' Salome comforted. 'Down ivy to ground, and go for doctor man.'

Clarissa regarded the black girl with undisguised amazement. 'Could you, Salome? Could you really reach the ground in safety from such a height?'

Salome bared her teeth in the wide, familiar smile, something she had not done for a very long while. 'You watch me, missus, please. I go like cat.'

Clarissa's eyes lit up as hope dawned. 'If that is the case, Salome, you could go down, re-enter the house and unlock this door. I do not think my husband has taken the key. As far as I know, it is still in the lock.'

Salome's black eyes were pitying. 'Oh, missus, why you not tell me that before? You doan know nothin'. Easier way than that. You got piece of paper?'

'Why, yes.' Clarissa rose to unlock her escritoire, from which she produced a letter. 'Will this do?'

By way of answer, Salome seized the letter, ran to the door and positioned the paper underneath it, near the keyhole. Then, extracting an ornamental bodkin from her hair, she poked at the keyhole until she heard the key drop with a satisfying plop. 'Hope it on paper,' she muttered, and gently pulled the letter back...minus the key. Salome made a noise of profound disgust, and prostrating herself in front of the door, endeavoured to catch sight of the key, emitting little grunts of effort and impatience. 'It no good, missus,' she said at last. 'I go down ivy.'

Before Clarissa could stop her, for she was having second thoughts about the advisability of such a manoeuvre, Salome was at the window, and having opened it, swung herself out by means of the ivy, stripped now of its red autumn leaves which had formed such a bright splash of colour on the side of the house. She was as good as her word. As she had claimed, she 'went like cat', and was on the ground before Clarissa could count to ten. Another five minutes sufficed to carry her to the outside of the bedroom door where she triumphantly pounced on the key.

Clarissa was already donning her cloak as Salome unlocked the door. 'You are to stay here, Salome,' she instructed, 'and lock yourself in. If any of the servants should come and knock, you are to tell them that the master has taken the key and that I am asleep. If they have brought food, tell them to take it back to the kitchens.

Say that I want nothing to eat until Mr Darker returns.'

Salome's eyes were round pools of curiosity. 'Where you go, missus?'

'To Lewes,' Clarissa answered. 'I could never face my child unless I had done all in my power to save Miss Pochin's life.'

'Maybe you come 'long too late,' suggested Salome with the fatalistic resignation of her race. 'You gonna ride horse? You shoulden ride horse fast case baby come.'

'There is no time to harness the gig,' Clarissa said, 'and in any case, Thomas Gander probably knows that I am forbidden to leave the house.' She added sarcastically, 'My husband seems to confide almost everything to that man.'

'He stop you taking horse, then,' Salome said flatly.

Clarissa's eyes flashed. 'Let him try!' She laid a hand on Salome's arm. 'When my baby comes, I swear I will do all that lies within my power to set you free. I swear it by my God.'

Salome nodded soberly. 'I know you keep promise, missus. You good woman.'

Clarissa, with a boldness belied by the

weak feeling in her knees, walked into the stable-court and ordered Tom Gander to saddle Sophie's second-best mare, 'Daisy'. Tom opened his mouth to argue the matter, then saw the look on Clarissa's face and, clamping his lips firmly together, proceeded to carry out her orders. God help me if anything befalls her, thought Tom grimly, as he tightened the saddle-girth. And devil take her for being a wayward bitch and disobeying her husband's commands. Ought to be whipped, did females who went against the wishes of their husbands. Tom gave the saddle-girth a last, irritable tug and turned wordlessly towards Clarissa, his cupped hands inviting her to mount. She did so, embarrassed by her own clumsiness and increased weight, and his so obvious observance of her condition.

Aware that the head groom was still watching her with a stern and brooding countenance, Clarissa walked Daisy out of the stable-court and into the gravelled driveway, kicking her into a trot as she passed under the arched gateway of the court with its little bell-tower. By the time she reached the main gates of Frinton Park, fortuitously open, the animal was at full gallop.

It was eight miles to Lewes and Clarissa passed few people on the road. Those she did paused in their progress to turn and stare at the fine lady who rode along as if Old Harry himself were after her. One gentleman, driving a light barouche, actually wheeled his horses, as if he purposed to set off in pursuit of her, but evidently thought better of it, and reining in his animal, sat with his hands on his knees staring after the flying horse and rider fast disappearing from view down the road.

Clarissa was within half a mile of her goal when a sharp cramping pain, low down in her abdomen, made her bend forward over the mare's neck. it seemed to take hold for a very long time, this iron claw gripping her insides, and the mare slowed down, sensing that her rider had lost control. Slowly, Clarissa straightened, took a deep breath, and exhaled it on a sigh of relief as the disagreeable sensation passed away. From then on she rode Daisy at a more sedate pace, but had scarcely gone more than another five hundred yards before the pain came back, forcing her over the mare's neck once more and driving the breath clean out of her body. This time the attack made her feel faint, and Daisy's glossy brown neck began to waver before her eyes. She made a tremendous effort to pull herself together, clinging like grim death to the bridle. By now she was approaching the outskirts of the town, and people were beginning to stop in their tracks and to gather in little knots, pointed excited fingers at her.

Despite her discomfort, Clarissa was miserably aware that she looked ridiculous. Daisy had slowed from a trot to a walk and now, all restraint gone, ambled to the side of the road to crop the grass. The wife of a Lewes shoe-maker, Mrs Leigh by name, possessed of more common sense and compassion than the other gapers, came up to this strange *equestrienne* and anxiously searched her face. 'Are you ill, ma'am?'

'The baby!' gasped Clarissa, white with shock.

'Mrs Darker, is it not?' inquired the woman with a start. She recognised Clarissa as having come to her husband's shop to buy pattens.

'Yes.'

'What in heaven's name are you doing, ma'am, riding a horse in your condition?'

'Please, the hanging...' Clarissa's voice tailed off as another spasm caught her unawares. Mrs Leigh looked even more amazed. 'Do you mean to tell me, ma'am, that you came all this way just to see a hanging, when you are so near your time?' Her air of astonishment was seasoned with a heavy pinch of disapproval.

'No, no..to...stop it,' Clarissa managed to gasp out. 'New evidence...'

'You are too late, then, ma'am.'

'Oh, no, no!' Clarissa started to weep, huddled over the mare's neck and holding on to her mane for dear life. 'Patience... dead? Oh, I cannot believe that such a terrible thing could have happened. Oh, God have mercy...'

'Not dead, ma'am,' Mrs Leigh said very loudly, forging her way through Clarissa's maze of agitation. '*Married,* ma'am. There was a gallows wedding. That's not occurred in these parts for fifty years or more.'

Clarissa slowly turned her head and stared at her rescuer. 'Married?' she repeated incredulously. 'Whom did she marry?'

Mrs Leigh shook her muslin-capped head. 'That I cannot tell you, ma'am. I can only repeat what I saw, which is little enough. There were three gentlemen, hatted and cloaked, who came up to the gallows tree just after they brought out the prisoner. Two of them pushed the third forward. 'Gallows wedding! Gallows wedding!' they shouted, and the chaplain, having asked the lady if she was prepared to be married in order to save her life, and having heard her signify assent, made the two handfast there and then.'

'What happened after that?'

Mrs Leigh shrugged her plump shoulders. 'They all made off together in a carriage driven by one of the other gentlemen.' Her brown eyes twinkled knowingly. 'If you ask me, ma'am, the gentleman who has made himself a bridegroom this day was not altogether willing. Ah, ma'am!' she exclaimed with anxious propriety, as Clarissa's head fell forward on to her breast, 'you are far from well.'

'Take me to the house of Mr George Branson at Southover...my uncle...' Clarissa managed to whisper. Mrs Leigh was just in time to catch her as she slid off Daisy's back.

Clarissa recovered consciousness to find Aunt Charlotte bending over her. The cramping pains in her stomach had abated somewhat, but she was instantly reminded of her plight by the large mound under the colourful patchwork quilt which covered her. 'The physician is coming, my dear,' Aunt Charlotte said, and stroked back her niece's tumbled hair with a gentle hand. 'How fortunate, is it not, that I am here to spend Christmas with George? I so like to make myself *useful.*'

'Dr Westlake?' murmured Clarissa, concerned only that the physician's familiar presence would soon materialise to help her.

'No, sweetheart,' Charlotte answered brightly, 'Dr Lyford. He lives here in the village.'

'Has Dr Westlake been sent for?'

Aunt Charlotte held her smile carefully in place. 'William is here, my dear. He will sit with you until Dr Lyford comes.'

At that moment William came in, smiling broadly, and pulled up a chair beside the bed. 'Well, my love,' he said with heavy jocularity, 'what an eventful day this has been. I rescue Cousin Patience from the gallows tree, drive her out of Lewes, and return to the "White Hart" for a glass, only to be informed by mine host that my wife has been taken ill. Mrs Leigh, sensible woman, left a message for me there.'

'Patience?' Clarissa queried feebly.

'Is now become Mrs Westlake...at least, for the time being.'

'I do not understand. Please, William, explain to me what has been going on.'

He took her hand, which lay like a quiescent and defenceless bird outside the quilt. 'Later, my dear, after...'

'No, *now!*' she insisted with surprising vigour. 'The baby will not be born for hours. I want to know *now.*'

William drew a deep sigh. 'So be it.'

She summoned up a weak smile. 'If the baby starts to come, I daresay you will be out of here faster than one of your hounds after a fox.'

'You may be sure of that,' he said, returning her smile. 'Well, let me see now.' He began to fidget, one hand playing a tattoo on his knees, the other scratching his nose reflectively. 'It is difficult to know where to begin. It would seem that our Dr Westlake is a scoundrel, a black-hearted villain, who will stop at nothing to further his career. What angers me more than I can say is that he has used my family for the furtherance of his own base designs.'

He had captured her interest. She shifted in the bed, offering up a prayer that the baby would be obliging enough to wait a little before breaking into their conversation. She said, 'I always liked him.'

'A-ha!' William chuckled grimly. 'I am sure he did his best to ensure that you held him in good esteem. It all started with Frances, you know.'

'Frances?' Her stare held both wonder and incredulity.

William's eyes were distant and a little sad. 'Yes. He hinted to me that she was too familiar with Richard, and that the child Frances carried might not be mine. Naturally, I taxed her with it, for the vile suggestion festered like a sore inside me, and having said my piece, quickly wished I could unsay it, for the look on her face will haunt me till my dying day. She did not say anything very much, neither denied nor confirmed the horrid insinuation, but the next thing I knew she had taken the stallion Richard gave her and was putting him at every fence she could find. The inevitable happened and she was thrown.

'I was not wholly to blame, God forgive me. Richard was always paying court to Frances, bringing her gifts, flattering her. She was a simple soul and saw no wrong in it.' He slapped his knee with his open palm and she saw the colour rush into his cheeks. 'There was no harm in it, and I should have known there was not, but a man is touchy where the honour of his wife is concerned.'

'Was Dr Westlake trying to make mischief, or did he really believe in the tale he told you?'

'Dr Westlake,' her husband replied steadily, 'once had the temerity to make a proposal of marriage to Frances, and he never forgave her for the manner of her refusal. She told him in no uncertain terms that he had looked too high.'

Clarissa frowned. 'Why did Frances keep him on as her physician after she married you? She must have despised him.'

'Yes, and that is where he was deuced clever. He apologised most humbly for his presumption, and never allowed her to see how greatly she had offended him. He was a good physician, I cannot deny that.

'After Frances died, he managed to convince me that he had acted in good faith, and Sophie had a fit of the vapours when I spoke of getting rid of him.' William massaged his forehead absent-mindedly. 'Now I come to think about it, I cannot understand how it was that the fellow had me so mazed that I could not see through him. Richard saw through him though, and made the mistake of baiting the fellow with such remarks as, "No, sir, I know that you would never presume to think that a fine lady would condescend to marry you." He almost paid for such indiscretions with his life.'

'Oh,' Clarissa said sadly, 'you are saying that Dr Westlake was responsible for the revenue men chasing Richard and Cornelius that night?'

Her husband nodded. 'He was.'

'How did you find out?'

William waved a careless hand. 'Cornelius made enquiries. It didn't take much ferreting out when a few palms were greased.'

'Why did you not tell me?'

William's look was suitably shamefaced. 'I misjudged you, my dear. As I said before, Frances was a simple soul, soft and very feminine, who liked everything to be decided for her. I thought you would be the same. I did not credit you with having much in the way of brains. I forbade anyone to tell you anything, in case the life of our child was put at risk.' A rueful smile followed this unflattering estimation of her character. 'As it is, I achieved just the reverse from what I had intended, because if I had told you all, you would not have embarked on that foolhardy ride. I am proud of you, Clarissa, for doing what you thought was right.'

Clarissa knew that she should have been pleased by her husband's openly expressed admiration for her. She could not explain to herself why she was not, or why his explanation was making her feel so depressed. She withdrew her hand from his and laid it across her stomach. 'Your child is safe, William. I am sure of it.'

He grinned and appeared not to notice the coolness of her tone. 'Little devil. I shall take him to task when he arrives for giving you a fright.'

'Or *she* arrives.'

'Or she,' he agreed equably. 'It matters not. I pray only that our child may be born alive.'

She groaned. 'It is alive, and punishing its poor Mama most cruelly.'

His eyes showed alarm. 'It is not...? Shall I see if the physician is coming?'

'No, please!' Her tone was frantic in its urgency. 'I must know about Patience.' She almost added '...in case I die', but refrained from doing so because she knew he would disapprove of such a sentiment. She asked, 'Did you investigate the truth of Mrs Clayton's evidence?'

'I did, though you thought me unfeeling and cruel.'

She retorted spiritedly, 'And so you were, to keep me in ignorance.'

'I shall not make the same mistake again if you will say that you forgive me.'

'I have no choice. Go on.'

The dry response occasioned a sharp look from William, who none the less proceeded with his tale. 'It appears that when our devoted saw-bones asked Patience to marry him he was in his cups, and later came to regret his rash proposal. He saw no way out of it though, until some devil prompted him to embroil her in a mess of trouble. She was not good enough for him, you see, this daughter of a humble lawyer's clerk, when his aim was to capture a lady of quality. No, no, it would not do at all, so the physician devised a scheme, bribing that rogue Smith to make it seem as if Patience had stolen the gloves from the Emporium. He planted your necklace in Patience's room, too. Must have done it on one of his frequent visits to Sophie, and I do believe he would have allowed his betrothed to hang if Cornelius and I had not thought up a little counter-scheme between us.'

William permitted himself a smile at his own cunning before continuing. 'We bearded the villain in his shop and forced him to confess to his deception—he did not take much persuading because he was half out of his wits with fright—and then we went to see our good friend the saw-bones, who, as you may suppose, was a different kettle of fish to deal with. He said it was Smith's word against his and that nobody would believe a runt like that, and *we* said they might if Mrs Smith testified to the fact that she had overheard her husband striking the bargain.

He chuckled reminiscently. 'That shook him considerable, as they say, especially since he didn't seem to know that a wife cannot testify against her spouse.

We pressed him a bit more, handing out threats which I doubt very much whether we could have put into commission, and then, when we had him softened up, we produced our trump card to the effect that we would not tell the justices what he had been up to, provided he agreed to marry Patience at a gallows wedding.'

Clarissa's hand plucked idly at the quilt. 'Which he did.'

'Aye. You heard that much, then?'

'Mrs Leigh told me.'

'Ah, yes...well, to continue, our saw-bones did not relish the prospect of becoming a bridegroom one bit, but he was like a coney in a trap, with Cornelius and me the only ones who could let him out. His spirits livened up when I said Patience would not hold him to his marriage-bond, and that he could see to an annulment as soon as may be, not, I added, purely for his own pleasure, but simply because Patience could not bear the sight of him after what he'd done to her.'

'"Does she know?" says he. "Of that you may be sure," says I, "and a right scoundrel she considers you to be." He did not like that either. Even after all that's gone, he values people's good opinion of him. He declares that he is for foreign parts. Good riddance, say I.'

'Where is Patience now?'

'Cornelius is taking her home to her father. I doubt very much whether we shall ever hear of her again, poor thing.'

'And I thought it was Sophie who had got her into trouble,' Clarissa said, and wondered why she did not feel contrite.

William made a sound of disgust. 'Do not waste your sympathy on Sophie. I'll admit to being a thought blind in that quarter. We have spoiled her shamefully, and it is time she grew up. I intend to find a husband for Miss Sophie, just as soon as may be, one who will knock the mischief out of her and the common sense in.'

'A marriage of convenience,' smiled Clarissa.

'You might say that. I am sure Cousin Patience thought her marriage mighty convenient, since it saved her from the rope.'

Clarissa shuddered. 'Poor Patience. It will be a long time before she recovers from an experience like that.'

The sound of carriage wheels sent

William running to the window. He peered through the small leaded panes. 'Dr Lyford,' he announced with a whistle of relief. 'I'll be off, then. Be a good girl now, and do what the saw-bones says.'

'I haven't much choice, have I?' Again she had stressed her inferior status, and again he refused to acknowledge the oblique protest. Returning to her side, he bent over her and kissed her cheek. 'I shall come and see you when it is all over.'

'If you are not too drunk.'

He smiled. 'A gentleman's privilege after the arrival of his first-born.'

She laid a restraining hand on his arm as he drew back. 'William, there is one more thing.'

'Yes?'

Had she imagined the note of wariness in his voice? She said, 'Something is bothering Salome. She is desperate to get away from Frinton Park.'

'Tom,' came the swift reply.

'What?'

'Tom Gander. He is the cause of her unease. It was Salome who put the dead cockerel near the mausoleum, because of some superstition of her own people that if someone dies as a result of betrayal, an offering must be made to propitiate the gods.'

'How did she know that the Countess was betrayed?'

'The Count...? Er, she did not, that is the odd part. She said that it was "something" told her so.'

'Odd indeed,' murmured Clarissa, who was quick to notice the stifling of a word half-said. 'Where does Tom come into it?'

'He caught her messing about with another cockerel and said that if she did not meet him somewhere after dark and pleasure him, he would tell me what she had been doing, and that I would shoot her.'

Clarissa was eyeing her husband with great speculation. 'I assume that Gander will be dismissed?'

William looked surprised. 'Why should I dismiss him? He is a good man with horses.'

She was about to ask yet another question when a wave of pain warned her that things were on the move again. William took one look at his wife and bounded out of the room, shouting for the physician to come up. Clarissa, struggling with the business of giving birth, reflected that men were deceitful, inconsistent creatures, and decided that sleeping dogs were best left to lie. It would be unwise of her to let William into a secret, namely that he was still under-estimating her intelligence, and that she knew his long and garbled explanation of recent strange events surrounding the Darker household to be compounded of a mixture of outright lies and half-truths. Frances Lacey a simple soul? Old Tom Gander—he who had never been known to look at a woman—a lecher? The cowardly Dr Westlake a stirrer up of evil passions? I shall never know the truth, thought Clarissa, but at least the final disaster has been averted and Patience is free as a bird.

Five hours later Clarissa gave birth to a premature son who was big enough for the physician to pronounce with confidence that he would survive. As promised, William came to see his wife. She smiled up at him weakly. 'Your breath does not reek of brandy.'

'A defect I am just about to remedy,' he said, and placed his lips on hers.

21

Young James Darker Is Christened

Clarissa sat with baby James in her arms, receiving the congratulations of her friends and relations. They came up, one after the other, to make odd noises at the baby, to smile fatuously or to embark upon lengthy reminiscences of their own first-born children, each according to his kind.

Aunt Charlotte puffed up on the arm of Cornelius. 'Just like his mother, my dear. Do you not agree, Mr Darker?'

Cornelius looked down at the baby. 'If you say so, ma'am, I am sure it is so.' He leaned over to peer rather more closely at the infant, whose little features were screwed up most disagreeably. 'Looks rather cross, don't he?'

'He is probably bored with watching us all eat and drink,' Aunt Charlotte said with a smile. 'Now come along, Cornelius, I am most anxious that you shall sample some of my brother's brandy. He has brought back twenty dozen bottles from his London vintners.' She lowered her voice conspiratorially, 'It will taste nothing like as good as our contraband variety, of course.'

Clarissa laughed as the unlikely pair moved off, and saw that Richard and Caroline were advancing upon her. She shifted the baby on to her other arm. At eight weeks he was becoming quite heavy. Caroline, perilously close to her own lying-in, sat down carefully beside her sister-in-law. 'Can I hold him?'

Clarissa smiled. 'Please do. My arm is aching.'

Caroline took the baby and kissed its forehead. 'Such a little love,' she crooned.

Richard, on leave from his regiment, was thinner than Clarissa remembered him. He smiled down at her. 'How is my nephew?'

'Extremely well, sir,' she answered, her manner reserved and formal. Clarissa could not rid herself of the feeling that Richard was responsible in part for the calamities of recent months. It always took something to spark off a chain of unhappy circumstances, and Richard, by his stubborn, arrogant flirtation with Frances, had supplied the first link in that chain, although the way in which the link had been forged was still unknown to her.

Richard seemed to sense Clarissa's slight animosity, but he was not unduly troubled by it. He shrugged lightly, as if to say, 'Dear sister, I care not a jot for your opinion of me,' and after running a finger across the child's smooth cheek, moved on. Immediately Caroline delivered up the baby to its mother and followed after her husband, throwing over her shoulder a vague, departing smile. They are well suited, Clarissa told herself, and cuddled baby James to her breast. He is like a wilful and spoilt child and she is content to treat him as such, hanging upon his every word, humouring his every whim. Marriage to Richard had changed Caroline. Now that she had him fast in the net she was continually on the alert lest he try and jump out of it.

Sophie, plate in hand, dumped herself unceremoniously beside mother and baby and chewed with great perseverance upon a piece of cheese-cake. She regarded Clarissa in the manner of an adversary sizing up the staying qualities of an opponent before saying abruptly, 'William says that he has granted Mr Briggs-Watson leave to pay court to me.' Mr Briggs-Watson was the son of a neighbouring farmer, a rather loud, brash young man, who hunted every season with such ferocity that one might well have imagined the fox to be his personal enemy. Clarissa thought him a very unpleasant personage, but no doubt William had his reasons for desiring Mr Briggs-Watson as a brother-in-law.

'We shall disagree every day,' Sophie claimed, 'and we shall fight like cat and dog, but I think that sort of thing adds spice to a marriage, do not you?'

Clarissa gave an involuntary shiver. 'I do not. I prefer a calm, ordered existence. Do you like Mr Briggs-Watson?'

Sophie's answering stare was markedly defensive. 'I like him well enough. I know him a great deal better than you knew William when you married him.'

Clarissa felt bound to counter this with, 'I have grown to respect your brother, Sophie. He is a very fine gentleman.'

Sophie explored the crevices of her teeth with one long fingernail, dislodging sundry strands of coconut which were tenacious in their efforts to stay put. 'Mr Briggs-Watson,' she said, 'is an only son. We shall be pretty comfortable, I think.'

'A marriage of convenience,' murmured Clarissa.

'Are not all marriages made for the convenience of both parties?' Sophie wanted to know, and flounced off to replenish her plate.

The baby started to make little chirping noises, a sure indication that he was working up an appetite. Clarissa was about to rise and repair to the nursery when the tall, bulky figure of her father appeared before her. 'Hold on, m'dear,' he cajoled. 'Just one little peep for grand-papa before the young gentleman is whisked from under my nose.'

Clarissa gave the baby to her father, who rocked him gently backwards and forwards in his strong arms and gazed lovingly upon the small, puckered face. 'Image of you, m'dear,' he said.

His daughter laughed. 'Nearly everyone on our side of the family says that James is the image of me, but the contrary is the case with the Darkers. They all think that he is like William.'

'Bit of both, I shouldn't wonder,' agreed Sir Charles tactfully. He sat down heavily on the sofa, still with the baby in his arms. 'It's turning out pretty well for you, Clarry, is it?' he asked, not without anxiety.

Her smile was bland and unrevealing. 'Yes, Father, very well indeed.'

Sir Charles gave a satisfied grunt. 'Thought that business over Cousin Patience and the saw-bones might have rocked the boat a bit.'

'It most certainly did that,' she replied with a tight little grimace.

'But you weathered the storm, eh?'

'Yes.'

'Arranged marriages,' said her father. 'They always turn out for the best. Let the youngsters have their heads and they'll gallop away to perdition most times.'

Clarissa held out her hands for the baby. Her amused eyes regarded Sir Charles with great affection. 'When shall you start thinking about a wife for little James, Father?' she asked.

He laughed wheezily. 'Next month will be soon enough, I should think.'

22

A Conversation Between Brothers

William stood face to face with his brother in the library. Beyond the closed doors the steady murmur of voices could be heard, increasing in volume sometimes as a vociferous christening guest mounted his favourite hobby-horse, sometimes erupting into laughter as a bawdy tale was unfolded out of range of the ears of the ladies.

'I have lately been wondering what became of our happy couple after you left them that morning,' said Cornelius, folding his arms across his chest and inspecting his perfectly rounded fingernails.

'They are probably over the water by now,' answered his brother. 'I made it pretty clear to our saw-bones friend that £3,000 is our top price to get him and his lady out of England for good. He'll not show his face in these parts again, at all events.' William terminated these words with a little grunt, and moving towards the shelves which housed volumes devoted entirely to foreign countries, took down several large tomes which he placed with a thump on his desk. A small cloud of dust rewarded his efforts.

'You were deuced lucky,' he observed, wiping the dirt from his fingers on the flaps of his frock-coat. 'It is not every man who will agree to become a scapegoat, and an outcast into the bargain.'

Cornelius shrugged. 'Where else would he get that much money? It would have taken him ten years to earn it here in Sussex. Now he will be able to purchase a thriving little practice in Germany or Holland, or wherever he takes the fancy to go.' He laughed unsympathetically. 'His first patient will be his bride, if I am any judge. When they brought her out she was gibbering like an idiot. I told her the day before that she should not hang if she agreed to our plan. It is my opinion that her brain went soft.'

'Yes, I noticed,' William answered dryly. 'The thought of dancing on air in front of a gaping crowd of some three or four hundred people should have been sufficient to concentrate her mind wonderfully. Instead, it seems to have had the opposite effect upon Cousin Patience. She was babbling away to the hangman as if her life depended upon it.' William frowned, and, selecting a book from the pile before him, flipped through the pages. 'What I have never been able to understand is how you became involved with Patience in the first place. You are generally more careful in such matters. Whores should be enjoyed well away from one's own hearthside. You should know that.'

Cornelius strolled over to a wall mirror and fussed with his hair. 'She was not exactly a whore. She was a quiet, respectable girl from a dull and impoverished home. She was...'—he searched for a word with an air of great concentration and found it at last—'innocent. I cannot stand gaudy, painted women, as you very well know. Let us say that she appealed to the more puritan side of my nature.'

William snorted with derision. 'She appealed to the more perverted side of your nature. Did you promise her marriage?'

The question astounded Cornelius. His plucked eyebrows shot heavenwards. 'Marriage? To a girl without a fortune? What a ludicrous suggestion.'

William seated himself at his desk and,

unlocking one of the drawers, drew forth a map which he unrolled, depositing two pewter ink-pots at either end of the heavy parchment to hold it down. 'I said did you *promise* her marriage.'

Cornelius was now arranging the fall of lace at his throat. 'Well, I may have hinted...to keep her docile, you know.'

'She must have quickly become disillusioned about that since she consented to marry Westlake.' William studied his brother's back view thoughtfully. 'Come to think of it, she seemed mighty pleased with herself after she became betrothed to Westlake. Could it be that she was relieved to have done with you?'

Cornelius did not turn round. 'If she was, she did not show it. She presented herself regularly at our trysting-places.'

'Or, perhaps,' suggested William, detecting a clear trace of defiance in his brother's tones, 'you forced her to meet you, holding her with the threat that you would tell Westlake about your liaison with her if she did not comply with your demands?'

The sudden stiffening in Cornelius's attitude told William all. 'Well, well,' he said, tracing with his finger the outline of the Windward Isles, 'you *have* been a rascal, Cornelius. At least I thought that the lady was willing, right up to the time she had the temerity to threaten to expose you over that unfortunate affair of the slave.'

'It was brilliant of *you,* William, to think up the idea of inculpating Patience in a felony,' Cornelius said with a touch of sarcasm.

William accepted the back-handed compliment with a reflective nod. 'Dashed odd, though, that Sophie should have beaten me to it. After the little drama which took place in Smith's Emporium, Miss Sophie shied like a frightened mare and confessed to me that she had put Clarissa's necklace in Patience's room in the hope that we would dismiss the wretched girl. I rebuked her handsomely and told her that if she held her tongue nothing more would be said. I intend to marry Sophie off as soon as may be to that oaf Briggs-Watson. He'll keep her out of mischief.'

Cornelius, having completed the admiring attentions to his person, ensconced himself in one of the library's deep, comfortable armchairs and, extracting a clay pipe and leather pouch from his pocket, began to fill the first with a golden brown mixture.

Laborious operations with a small tinder-box and steel culminated in the successful application of flame to tobacco, and he was soon puffing away enjoyably and watching William's finger-explorations of the map.

'Patience,' William said slowly, forefinger idling along the west coast of Santo Domingo, 'was a very foolish young woman to suppose that she could put the family's good name in question. The threat, I take it, was offered to induce you to leave her be?'

Cornelius nodded and blew out a stream of smoke which curled away and upwards, until it disappeared into the elegant intricacies of the Adam-style ceiling. William was looking at him curiously. 'Was it Patience who set the revenue men on to you? You never did say?'

Cornelius laughed. 'Yes. I think she hoped to have me removed from the scene long enough to be able to marry Dr Westlake and establish herself as a respectable matron.'

'Poor wretch.'

A careless shrug greeted this weak expression of sympathy. 'She asked for all she got. That meek sort always do.'

'The meek sort, as you put it, can turn very nasty in the end,' William said, 'as you might have discovered to your cost. As it is, things nearly went wrong when Clarissa took a fit of the vapours after the trial. I should have lost another child if you had not hit upon the idea of a gallows wedding. Even then our young man was born before his time.'

Cornelius, gazing ruminatively at the ceiling and admiring his delicate blue smoke-rings, went off on another tack. 'I thought it was Patience who was putting the cockerels on the steps of the mausoleum, indulging in a kind of childish revenge, and then it turned out to be Salome practising some voodoo mumbo-jumbo over that dead black.'

William, absorbed once more in his map, looked up with a half-smile. 'I told Clarissa that it was Tom Gander who had been at the girl.'

Cornelius's eyebrows lifted. 'That old eunuch? Did she believe you?'

William grimaced and unconsciously echoed his wife's words. 'She had no choice.' He went on. 'I am sending Salome away. Clarissa thinks I am going to find her husband and children for her, so keep a still tongue in your head. I mean to sell her to a man over at Brighthelmstone. He wanted a good children's nurse, and is willing to pay me a handsome sum for her.'

Cornelius asked, 'What did you tell Clarissa about Patience?'

'I gave her a long and garbled explanation, composed of truth and lies, mostly lies I must admit, and branding Westlake as the villain of the piece. I left your name out of it entirely, except to say that it was Westlake who had betrayed you to the revenue men.'

'That's good!' Cornelius brightened and looked relieved. 'I like Clarissa. I should not care for her to lose her good opinion of me.'

'She'll do,' agreed William, 'though I must admit that her head is filled with mighty strange notions at times. Notions of female equality with men, notions that blacks are as good as whites, and such-like nonsense. She will be with child again in no time at all, of course, and I intend to keep her that way for as long as possible. It is the only way with women. Stuff their bellies in order to unstuff their heads.'

This coarse philosophy amused Cornelius no end. He belched forth a combination of smoke and laughter. 'Does she know that you killed Frances?'

William did not recoil with horror at this coolly posed question, but managed none the less to assume a creditable air of outraged innocence. 'You know very well that I did not kill Frances. What an idea.'

'You chased her with a riding crop over three miles of land, taking nineteen hedges on the way, until she fell and killed herself and the baby.'

'I did *not* kill her.' William insisted. 'She killed herself. I was chasing her to administer a beating which she richly deserved. The child she carried was not mine. It was Richard's. Frances was a whoring bitch.'

'You did not want that child,' Cornelius accused. 'You hoped that Frances would die.'

'What if I did?' challenged his brother. 'I have a right to expect that the fruit of *my* loins shall inherit *my* land, and any woman who deceives her husband as Frances deceived me deserves such a fate.'

'Patience saw you chasing after Frances. She told me so. She was botanising in the woods when you both dashed by.'

William gave an amused chuckle. 'I found out afterwards that it was her, although I could not be sure at the time.'

'She knew you had something more on your mind than simply fetching your wife back home. She said that you had murder written on your face.'

'I know. She was stupid enough to accuse me to my face of frightening Frances to death. I put her in her place, but our relationship was never the same after that. From then on she was just one of the servants to me.'

'So you have more than one reason for hounding her?'

'Yes.'

The expression on his brother's face caused Cornelius to think that it would be wise to change the subject. 'I truly believe that Clarissa might be so foolish as to fall in love with you,' he remarked. 'I think you have tamed her.'

William smiled. 'Yes, I think I have.' He beckoned to his brother. 'Come over here and look at this.' He stabbed at the map with his forefinger. 'Captain Gomez says that there are some very fine bucks and females on this island here,'—the finger came to rest on a small dot off Santo Domingo. 'Since Daddy Jones is becoming so niggardly...forgive the pun...over terms, it might be a good idea to investigate fresh fields. What do you think?'

Cornelius studied the map. 'It is a good idea,' he approved, 'just so long as you do not expect me to inspect the cargo. Deuced unpleasant people, those savages.'

'Salome is a savage,' William said with a grin.

'Yes, well...' Cornelius scratched his nose. 'Salome has been cleaned up a bit since you bought her.'

The brothers, heads together, planned their next foray into slave-trading.

23

Dr And Mrs Westlake

It is necessary, for the purposes of this narrative, to go back in time to that fateful day in mid-December when Dr Westlake and his bride were bundled into a post-chaise and left to their own devices. The newly-married pair rode the eight miles to Brighthelmstone, and then went on by hired carriage to the port of Newporth; a hired carriage, with its superior comforts, was a mode of conveyance more suited to the physician's recently-acquired affluence.

The journey was a long and silent one, for the expression on Mrs Westlake's stubbornly averted face never once softened into acceptance, and her eyes never lost their look of blank disinterest in the passing scene.

An attempt at conversation on the part of the physician was almost totally ignored, though the bloodless lips of the young woman did manage to form some sort of unintelligible monosyllable from time to time. He was not the man to persist in the face of such unequivocal hostility. In truth, he had much to think about, and it was perhaps fortunate that his bewildered brain was not called upon to formulate the meaningless expressions requisite for polite social intercourse.

It was taking Robert Westlake a long time to reach a satisfactory conclusion regarding the attitude he should adopt towards his present circumstances. Indeed, if he ever did reach any conclusion at all he was not aware of it. Anger, inextricably bound up with elation, invaded his mind, and he was totally unable to separate the two in order to determine which was the stronger. Elation reposed in the inside pocket of his waistcoat in the guise of a note for £3,000 drawn upon the bank of Messrs Coutts of London. It was an extraordinarily gratifying sum, which only a man of absurdly high principles could have refused. Anger, on the other hand, was inherent in the fact that he had, to put it vulgarly, been bought off by the gentry, to whom he had sold his good name and any hope of a future as a physician in England. When Cornelius Darker had approached him with his startling proposition Robert Westlake begged leave to wonder why the Darker brothers should be so concerned about the life of a convicted felon, especially one towards whom they had never displayed anything more than a kind of contemptuous tolerance. With an air of pious rectitude which had done nothing to deceive the other man, Cornelius had explained that his distressing affair had so upset Mrs Darker that Mr Darker feared for the life of his unborn child if Miss

Pochin were to suffer the fate which her crime merited.

Dr Westlake, who had then asked politely if he might have at least a day or two in which to consider the proposal put to him, showed his visitor out with a sense of puzzlement which he did not permit the younger Mr Darker to discern upon his blandly smiling features, but his thoughts were his own, and he could not help wondering just what sort of *imbroglio* he was getting himself mixed up in. Doubts about his betrothed's guilt had begun to penetrate his mind, and he had come very close to the truth in supposing that she had done something to offend the Darker family, something heinous enough to prompt them to hound her to death.

It might very well be true that Mrs Darker's delicate condition had forced them to take pause at the eleventh hour and hatch up this scheme to be relieved of Miss Pochin's presence in less drastic fashion. Mrs Darker, the physician knew, was an intelligent and determined woman, and she had never believed Patience Pochin to be a thief.

As the carriage swayed and jolted along over the sticky, rutted road, which had not yet dried out after the autumn rains, Dr Westlake sneaked a glance at his wife, and was coldly chilled by the knowledge that he remained in ignorance of a great deal of pertinent information. Time and patience alone might bring him to the heart of the mystery.

Mrs Westlake's thoughts, meanwhile, were as disordered as those of her husband, towards whom she now experienced a deep revulsion. He had not believed in her innocence, and for that she could never forgive him. Conscience reminded her that she had, in fact, grossly deceived him over the matter of her affair with Cornelius Darker, an affair which had started as a marvellous idyll and had turned into black nightmare. She would have married the physician with the lie in her heart, and for that God had punished her.

Her mind conjured up a picture of Cornelius coming to her cell on the day before she was to be hanged, standing there propped indolently against the wall, smiling down at her and outlining his plan for her salvation. 'It will be as if all this had never happened, my dear Patience. You will become Westlake's wife, a fate infinitely to be preferred to that which awaits you in the morning.'

Watching that false smile, which had never left his face as he spoke, she had longed to rake her dirty fingernails down his cheeks, to erase its stinging mockery, and to bring even a tiny measure of pain to one who had inflicted so much upon her. She had clung desperately to what dignity remained to her, and had managed to say coolly, 'I marvel, sir, that you do not offer yourself as the gallows bridegroom. It would be more fitting, would it not, since you have already enjoyed my favours?'

It had been a pathetic attempt to appeal to the better side of his nature, a mere pin-prick which caused him not a moment's unease. The smile on his face had broadened as he replied, 'Oh, I am sure you are right, ma'am, but I fear that my affections are now engaged elsewhere. Miss de Lisle of Upton Hall has done me the honour to consent to become my wife on the seventeenth day of April next year. Under the circumstances, you will not expect to receive an invitation to the festivities?'

'You might have spared me that.' The words had almost choked her. She had turned away her head so that she might not see the gloating eyes bent so relentlessly upon her. How she had longed to make the grand gesture and refuse to accept him as her deliverer, but it would have taken a woman of infinitely higher courage than she to embrace the hangman's rope as an alternative to contracting a loveless, humiliating match with a man she now utterly despised.

Cornelius had left her seated at the table with her head sunk upon her arms, weeping bitterly, her unwilling brain conjuring up memories of the first days of her betrothal, when she had walked about in a daze of relief and delight, her only worries pecuniary ones, her only decisions relating to the advisability or otherwise of making a particular purchase.

The next morning, when the gaoler had arrived to unlock the door of her cell, and the chaplain had thumped in in his heavy boots to prepare her soul for the unknown, she had gone through the grisly ritual still with fear clutching at her stomach, because it was just possible that Cornelius had lied to her about Mrs Darker's distress, that he had come merely to turn the handle of the rack a little further, to give her hope, only to snatch it away. The prayers of the chaplain had receded into unintelligible mumbles as the terror within her mounted, took complete possession of her, penetrated into the furthest extremities of her body, and finally came to rest upon her tongue, which began to babble incoherencies at an alarming rate. They thought her reason was deserting her, and had debated whether or not to dose her with laudanum. The chaplain, lips slavering with anticipation, had been against the administration of anything which would 'dull the prisoner's realisation of the terrible crime she had committed, and remit the exigencies of the just punishment meted out by the law for such a fall from grace', but agreed that word should be despatched immediately to the hangman that he was about to be handed a troublesome victim.

They had led her out, still chattering, on to the scaffold, which she mounted directly in front of the open prison door, to be confronted by a sea of upturned, curiously expressionless faces. Pale, blurred ovals, they reminded her of the faces of the damned as depicted on the mural in Piddingfold parish church, that same church she had hoped to attend as a happy bride.

The fact that she was to be rescued had buried itself out of reach in the dim recesses of her brain, and all she could think of now was that those merciless eyes might see up her skirts as she swung back and forth above them. Quickly, she had torn the kerchief from about her neck and fumblingly attempted to tie her legs together below her knees, while the crowd, wickedly astute, roared their approval of such modesty. The hangman, more humane than those who would have shrunk before offering to perform his office, had taken the kerchief from her hand to carry out this small service for her. Then he had carried her to the spot where she must stand. The noose, neatly and expertly prepared, hung slightly above the level of her eyes. She would never know what had prompted her to pull it down about her neck. Again the crowd had roared their appreciation, while she fingered the rough hemp and felt the fibres prick her hands. She had seen the hangman advancing towards her, a black bag held before him, and suddenly faintness had overcome her. There had been a confused buzzing noise in her ears, above which could barely be heard the voice of a man shouting. Swiftly, she had turned her head, blindly questing for the source of the voice as it became clear to her that the possibility of deliverance did indeed exist, and so it had proved. The words had soon become distinguishable...'Gallows wedding! Gallows wedding!'

A minute or so later the chaplain, cheated of his fun, had surlily intoned the marriage service, while the crowd watched, entranced, the spectacle taking place before them of a bride, whose neck was encircled by a rope, being joined in holy matrimony to a man disguised by hat and cloak into suspicious anonymity. Within ten minutes of mounting the scaffold the prisoner had been a free woman, and had been driven away in a carriage.

What now, pondered Mrs Westlake, remarking the fields, still bare after the autumn harvest, sliding by. She considered the possibility of spending the future in some foreign town, where she knew neither the language nor the customs of the people. The idea, for one of her peculiarly English upbringing, was too terrible to contemplate. Bound for ever to a man she hated, she would exist in a dreary vacuum which had no sense or meaning.

Mrs Westlake, tired beyond feeling, closed her eyes against the dreary afternoon landscape, and drifted into an uneasy doze.

24

Mrs Westlake Examines a Pistol And Dr Westlake Goes To Amsterdam

The bride and 'groom spent their wedding-night in a splendid hostelry situated at the junction of the turnpike road between Newporth and London. Not surprisingly, they made no confession concerning their newly-wedded status, and after passing the night in distant wretchedness, she upon the bed and he upon a low divan, went in search of lodgings.

The physician confided to his silent wife that he intended to stay in the little port for several weeks while he made the necessary inquiries concerning a post abroad. Holland, he thought, since there was more scope for a keen medical practitioner in that country. The Dutch physicians, he remarked, were far more knowledgeable in the science of medicine than were their French and German counterparts. This information elicited nothing more than an almost imperceptible shrug from Mrs Westlake, whose attention became inextricably engaged by a passing barouche.

It being out of season, the physician and his wife quickly found an apartment suitable for their temporary needs in a villa overlooking the sea. The apartment was situated on the first floor, and Mrs Westlake very quickly established the habit of positioning herself in an armchair before the window, whereupon her gaze would instantly become riveted on the variety of small craft which daily went about their business on the crowded stretch of water known as the English Channel. Occasionally, a man o' war, coming in to be refitted at Shoreham, engaged her interest, and by dint of straining her ears, she could hear the shouts of the sailors as they swarmed up the rigging and busied themselves with multifarious tasks on deck.

It disturbed her husband not a little to notice that her hands remained unemployed while she pursued this seemingly pointless exercise, and that his tentative suggestions regarding the purchase of linen and embroidery silks, or perhaps some tatting cotton, were acknowledged briefly, and then totally ignored. The hands remained obstinately idle, neatly folded on the green skirt.

The Westlakes' culinary requirements being catered for by the landlady, the physician did not even have the satisfaction of hearing his wife busying herself with pots and pans, the homely clatter of which might have offered him some comfort, and it was not long before Patience Westlake's almost total withdrawal from him began at first to irritate, and then to move him to anger.

He made a private resolve to allow her no longer than six months in which to recover from her unfortunate experiences. After that he would demand not only his conjugal rights, but also his right to a little pleasant conversation. He did not intend to spend the rest of his life with a wooden puppet, for it had already occurred to him that he certainly could not beget children upon an object so lacking in animation. In the meantime, he prescribed certain medicaments for her, which she took without a murmur of protest, and bided his time, reflecting wryly that no marriage could ever have begun with less chance of success.

On an evening in March, after Dr and Mrs Westlake had resided in Newporth for upwards of three months, the physician sat at the table in the withdrawing-room engaged upon writing a reply to a gentleman in Amsterdam who had a medical practice for sale. According to the Dutch gentleman, his clientele included one grand-duke and two counts, and he estimated the revenues of the practice at some 15,000 guilders per annum. These claims Dr Westlake took with a substantial pinch of salt, but decided nevertheless that the matter would bear investigation. He therefore stated in his letter that he would be honoured to pay a visit to Amsterdam on the twenty-fourth day of March.

Putting aside his pen, the physician was suddenly struck by the idea that he might need protection on so hazardous a journey, and that it would be as well to see that his pistols were in good working order. These last were kept in a polished mahogany box of some antiquity which had once belonged to Robert Westlake's maternal grandfather, a sergeant in the 18th Lancers who had distinguished himself in the rising of 1715.

The pistols which now reposed in the box had not, in fact, belonged to this military gentleman, but Dr Westlake liked to pretend that they had, and that they had been the silent witnesses of many a dawn *recontré,* arranged to defend the honour of some noble lady. In sober reality they had been made by Messrs Forsyth of London for an impecunious young subaltern who had later been forced to put them in pawn. The subaltern's tempestuous career precluding the possibility of his ever being able to redeem his property, they had been snapped up by Dr Westlake, whose keen eye surmised correctly that they were the very size to fit snugly into the mahogany box.

Having placed the box with reverent self-deception on the table in front of him, the physician unfastened the brass clasps and disclosed to view two extremely fine matching pistols of the four-barrelled volley variety, with brass frame and barrels. Not even the wildest flight of imagination could have pronounced these exquisitely fashioned instruments as having been made for the purposes of duelling. They were strictly for military use. Fortunately for Dr Westlake, none of those persons of his acquaintance to whom he had shown the pistols, with pride swelling in his heart, had possessed enough expertise on the subject of firearms to challenge their owner's claims.

The physician extracted a pistol from the box and with deft, slim fingers unscrewed one of the barrels near the breech. He had barely begun upon the second before he became aware, more by instinct than by observance, that he was being watched.

He swung round quickly, and was amazed to see that the spectacle of ocean and boats, fast disappearing in the deepening twilight, no longer engaged his wife's attention. She had turned in her chair and was regarding him with an expression of grave interest.

'What are you doing?'

Here is progress indeed, thought the physician with a feeling of triumph. She has spoken four consecutive words to me! He thought it best not to allow his satisfaction to show, however, and answered quietly, 'I am about to clean my pistols. If I am to go to Amsterdam to see our Dutch friend I prefer to go armed.'

This statement elicited no response from her, and he had begun to think that she had said all she intended to say on this occasion when, with a rustle of silk petticoats, she rose from her chair and came to stand beside the table. Her hand went out and extracted the second pistol from its velvet nest. She balanced it on her palm, estimating its weight. The act, indicating as it did a certain professionalism, made him smile. He said, 'They are very fine duelling pistols.'

'They are military pistols,' she contradicted calmly, 'made by the Forsyth factory, I believe. My uncle, who served in the 9th Foot, had one very similar to this.'

He was staring at her with a mixture of indignation and surprise, and for the first time since that dreadful morning outside Lewes gaol she smiled, but it was a smile which did not reach her eyes. She said, 'How very little we know of each other.'

'There was scarcely time,' he mumbled and fell silent.

'The best way to clean pistols is with

palm oil,' she instructed coolly. 'Do you possess any?'

He shook his head, and she shrugged. 'The ironmongers in Milton Street will have some.'

'Yes.' It astonished him that the ironmonger's establishment in Milton Street had even come to her notice, so apathetic had been her demeanour on the rare occasions when they had walked out together.

'Have you the means to load the pistols?'

Wordlessly, he slid open a small drawer let into the base of the box and revealed a brass power horn and a dozen balls. She stared critically at these articles for a moment or two and then appeared to lose all interest in the weapons. Discarding that which was in her hand, she returned to her chair and assumed her former, withdrawn pose. He fiddled with the pistols a while longer, but her unexpected intervention had somewhat unnerved him, and it was not long before he returned them to the box and the box to its place on the chiffonier. Then, thinking that the spell might be broken at last, he attempted further conversation, but his paltry offerings were spurned as firmly as before. Sullenly, he settled down to read.

On the twenty-fourth day of March, Dr Westlake kept his appointment with Dr Huyt of Amsterdam, and was agreeably surprised, not to say astounded, to discover that he had been told the exact truth concerning the practice. It was thriving, and a bargain at the price suggested by the Dutchman. Despite having been honoured with an appointment as physician to the Prince of Orange, Dr Huyt was loth to give up his practice. He was a homely, down-to-earth sort of man who preferred to deal with commoners, but when royalty commanded...here the voluble little physician had produced an expressive shrug indicative of his helplessness in the face of regal patronage.

Dr Westlake, well pleased with the results of his excursion, boarded the Newporth packet, nurturing the faint hope that his wife would summon up at least a show of enthusiasm for the news he had to impart. In this he was doomed once again to disappointment, for when he arrived back at their lodgings she was nowhere to be found. The landlady, hurriedly called up, informed him cheerfully that Mrs Westlake, who had admitted to feeling lonely and bored, had decided to visit her father at Hounslow, and had left the apartment two days ago for that very purpose, taking with her a small valise.

Dr Westlake allowed himself to appear satisfied with this explanation, but when the landlady had gone, he was unable to dismiss a distinct feeling of unease. His wife's sudden decision to visit her father was not commensurate with her morose state of mind. He felt very sure, from his own recent experiences, that she had little desire to communicate with any living creature, least of all those to whom she was connected by ties of blood.

The physician was in a quandary. The thought occurred to him that his wife might well be in a suicidal frame of mind, and had left home in order to do away with herself by plunging into the sea, or perhaps... The thought that now entered his head sent him flying to his box of drugs. A quick search revealed that neither his bottle of laudanum nor his box of opium pills was missing. He confessed to himself that this meant little, since a few coppers would purchase enough of those dangerous substances to do away with a regiment. The physician moved about the apartment in a state of indecision, rejecting his first impulse to go to Hounslow in order to verify his wife's whereabouts. If she were not there he would have had a wasted journey, and if she were, their peculiar circumstances and her refusal to communicate with him might cause a great deal of embarrassment all round.

Having unpacked his bag, Dr Westlake completed the disposal of his possessions by replacing the pistol which had accompanied him to Amsterdam in its mahogany box. He was about to close down the lid of the box when, in one of those delayed flashes of recognition which most people experience at one time or another, his brain confirmed that the pistol's fellow was missing. The physician stared down at the outline of the weapon, deeply indented in red velvet, for a long time, before muttering, half to himself, 'She is going to do away with herself. I think I knew it from the very moment I discovered that she was gone.'

Robert Westlake sat for a full hour over his glass of port that night, and eventually came to the conclusion that he must allow events to take their course.

If fortune smiled on him his wife's body might never be identified, and he would be free for ever from an embarrassing encumbrance.

25

Cornelius Darker Is Married

Cornelius Darker's bride was sixteen, charmingly pretty, devoid of brain-power, and in possession of an extremely large fortune. Even William was impressed by the size of it. 'If Miss de Lisle and her family had come into the county eighteen months ago,' he told his brother jocularly, 'you'd not have stood a chance against my superior powers of persuasion.'

Cornelius signified his appreciation of this quip with loud laughter and laid one forefinger alongside his nose. 'You should have become a member of the smuggling fraternity, William. I have been known to range far and wide to establish my contacts, and have encountered a great many interesting people.'

'Sir Anthony de Lisle was one of your customers, I suppose?'

Cornelius frowned unconvincingly and said with mock indignation, 'Sir, surely you do not expect me to reveal the names of my erstwhile clients to the son-in-law of a magistrate?'

William chuckled and flung his arm about his brother's shoulders. 'If you want any slaves,' he offered, 'I have a fresh shipment awaiting disposal in London. Just say the word.'

A mental vision of the new home bought for the happy couple by the bride's father swam before Cornelius's intoxicated eyes. A fine mansion, set in one hundred acres of parkland, would require a large number of servants, and if some could be obtained without the necessity of having to pay wages, he was not the man to pass up such an opportunity. 'I'll take a couple of bucks,' he told his brother.

'What about a female?' William asked.

Cornelius produced a prodigious wink. 'Perhaps I shall take one from the next consignment. I've enough woman-flesh to occupy my time and energies for the next six months or so.'

William's eyes narrowed. 'Be kind to

her at first,' he warned. 'Remember that tonight you will be taking a schoolgirl to your bed, not a whore. It would be a thought disconcerting if she complained to her Mama of your exuberance between the sheets.'

'What if she does?' Cornelius said, with the quick frown of a small boy who thinks he has been unfairly rebuked. 'She will be my property, and I shall do as I please with her.' Cornelius was still wallowing in a flood of euphoric delight resultant upon the capture of so valuable a prize as Miss Elizabeth de Lisle, whose father, while viewing somewhat askance the prospect of bestowing his daughter upon the youngest brother of a gentleman farmer, had become ensnared by the seductive offer of a half-share in a new slaver which William Darker was having built at Buckler's Yard in Hampshire. Everything, as far as Cornelius was concerned, was set fair for the future. If only someone would get up the nerve to kick the trouble-making Abolitionists out of Parliament his happiness would be complete.

Young Parson Ellsworth, standing in for the regular incumbent, who at that very moment was shivering in bed with a quartan ague, could not conceal the fact that he was painfully nervous. He gabbled through the marriage service, making several mistakes, and crowned his incompetence by demanding to know in a shaking voice 'if anyone here present knew of any just cause or impediment why these two persons should not be joyfully loined in holy matrimony.'

Irreverent and unsuppressed mirth rippled round the tiny church, almost bringing the ceremony to an abrupt halt, but Parson Ellsworthy, his cheeks a-flame with humiliation, stumbled on to the conclusion, and with sweat breaking out from every pore in his body, pronounced Cornelius Darker and Elizabeth de Lisle man and wife.

Pandemonium broke out in the church as the wretched man's *faux pas* was remarked upon, jeered at, and lengthily discussed, and order was not restored until Cornelius and his bride returned from signing the parish register and began to walk at a fairly smart pace down the aisle. The bridal couple had just drawn level with the Darker family pew when a shot rang out, shockingly loud above the murmurs of admiration for the little bride's joyful countenance, and the bridegroom sank slowly to his knees, clutching at his breast, where a bloom of red had appeared to mar the perfection of his white brocade waistcoat. There were shouts of outrage from the gentlemen and shrieks of horror and dismay from the ladies, and all heads were turned instantaneously towards the west door, before the opened portals of which there stood outlined the figure of a woman, garbed in black, and heavily veiled. In her right hand she held a smoking pistol.

Too stunned by surprise to make a move, the open-mouthed congregation continued to stare at the woman as she calmly revolved the barrel of the pistol and pointed it with a steady hand at the figure of William Darker, who knelt by the side of his dying brother. A second shot rang out, but the assassin's aim was impaired as Harry Lambton, the first of those present to be galvanized into action, sprang at her and struck up her arm. As he did so his elbow became entangled with the heavy gauze veil. Inadvertently, he jerked it aside, and in doing so pulled off the lady's hat, disclosing to view the ghastly, pallid features of Mrs Westlake.

'Miss Pochin!' gasped Harry, and, quite forgetting she was armed, he loosed his hold upon her. In a trice she had revolved the barrel of the pistol yet again and had turned it upon herself, but before her finger could squeeze the trigger, William, who had raced down the aisle to aid in the securing of her person, wrenched it from her grasp. Then, throwing back his arm, he dealt her a resounding blow on the ear which snapped back her head. In a voice as cold as ice he said, *'You will hang now, ma'am. I promise you that!'*

She began to weep, and fell on her knees before him, while the wedding-guests looked on in startled fascination, and the bride watched her husband draw his last breath with incredulous eyes.

'Please!' Her hands came up to claw at his legs. 'Let me do away with myself. Do not make me go through all that horror again. Have you no pity, sir?'

'None!' he assured her through clenched teeth, and pulled her to her feet. His hold upon her was not fast enough, however, and before he could stop her she had torn herself away and was running down the aisle towards the pulpit. Picking up her skirts, she mounted the little spiral staircase to the lectern. The open Bible exhorted her to turn the other cheek. She read the familiar words with a smile, and seeing her smile the wedding-guests thought she must have taken leave of her senses. Their upturned faces reminded her vividly of that other occasion—was it only four months ago?—when she had climbed some wooden steps and then looked down. This time she would make a farewell speech. Her head lifted, and in ringing tones she addressed them:

'Hear me, good people of Piddingfold. This day true justice has been done, for I have killed the man who seduced me.'

A horrified murmur ran through the congregation, but her voice rose above it and her finger pointed at the crumpled and bloody heap in the nave, where the remains of the man who had wooed her, seduced her, used her and tortured her for two long years, moved no more.

'That vile man bought my body with a promise of marriage, and it was many months before I discovered the depths to which he could sink, that he was a lecher and a murderer, who thought nothing of beating a slave to death and burying his body without benefit of clergy. When I threatened to expose him he bribed Mr Smith, the haberdasher, to involve me in a theft.'

Her voice rose, hovering on the brink of hysteria. 'it was only because Mr Darker's wife showed herself to be a woman of charitable instincts that I was spared.'

Her eyes, wild as those of a frightened horse, sought out the pale, shocked face of Clarissa, who was already pregnant with her second child. 'Mrs Darker!' she exclaimed, her hands gripping the edge of the pulpit as though it were a life raft tossing in the midst of a stormy sea. 'Your husband feared that you might miscarry because of your compassion for my plight. It was he who arranged for me to go free. He is as guilty as that other. You have married a monster, and you live amongst a nest of monsters!' The last word was hurled forth on the wings of a demented scream before the distraught woman slumped forward over the edge of the pulpit in a dead faint.

It was William Darker who now took charge of the proceedings, ushering the wedding-guests out of the church, bidding the parents of the widowed bride to carry her off as soon as may be, arranging for the disposal of his dead brother's body, and for the constables to arrest the murderess and take her once again to Lewes gaol, all under the bewildered eyes of his wife, whose hand was as cold as ice as he handed her to her carriage and sent her home.

As the Darker's coachman whipped up the horses Clarissa saw the blood bespattered bride being bundled into a closed barouche, leaving behind her a posy of bright spring flowers which was swooped upon by a little girl and carried off in triumph.

Harry Lambton, riding hell-for-leather to fetch the constables from the village, passed her on the road, and she pictured Patience, surround by a ring of hostile faces as she waited for a terrible fate to overtake her for the second time. She had suspected all along, of course, that William had not told her the truth. What she had not suspected was the illicit liaison between the seemingly carefree, amusing Cornelius and his lowly cousin, with William presumably conniving at the relationship and going to the length of jeopardising the life of an innocent woman in order that the good names of himself and his brother might not disappear under the lash of slanderous tongues.

How can I go on living with such people, Clarissa asked herself, and knew, even as the question formed itself in her mind, that the alternative would be bleak indeed. Willingly would her father take her back into the house of her childhood, but not all the generosity of Sir Charles's kind heart could make up for a life spent apart from her children, whom William would lay claim to, as he would to any of his possessions which were in danger of being taken from him.

She would live the life of a lonely spinster while her children grew to maturity and quickly forgot that they had ever had a mother. William, she knew, would never suffer as a result of his brother's shortcomings. Patience's outburst in the church would be explained away as the lying ravings of a spiteful woman, her murder of Cornelius as an act of savagery for which no punishment could prove too harsh. 'This time you will hang,' she had heard William say, and doubted not for one moment that he spoke the truth.

Tied to Clarissa's wrist by a silken

ribbon was a bag of rose petals which she had brought to strew before the bride and 'groom as they came out of the church...to bring them luck. With a sudden feeling of revulsion she wrenched the bag from her wrist, and pulling down the window of the carriage, threw it out. The cool breeze fanned her face, and she rested her head against the padded interior of the coach. 'Dear father,' she murmured, 'what think you now of your marriage of convenience?'

26

Clarissa Comes To Terms With Life

'How dare you, ma'am!' William's voice should have made her quake with fear, but she had never felt so calm in her life. His fists pummelled the empty air. 'How dare you buy back that woman's body from the anatomists and put it in *my* mausoleum!'

Deliberately, she kept her voice low. 'Your mausoleum contains quite a few guilty secrets, does it not, William? I should not have thought one more would have unduly disturbed the other occupants.'

'Explain your meaning, ma'am!' He was being more than usually pompous, and his stare was angry and accusing. She met it without flinching. 'I have heard the villagers say that you hounded poor Frances to death because she was unfaithful to you, and that Patience was a witness to your murderous intent.'

His face was congested with fury. 'They would not dare! They would not dare say such a thing to you!'

'Not directly,' she agreed, still with that maddening air of superiority, 'but one does hear rumours.' She added without pause, 'There is also the matter of the slave, Tolko, who has found a resting place in the garden of the mausoleum. Salome made sacrifices for him, did she not? She was not concerned for the soul of a mere Christian. The Countess was "one of them", while the slave was "one of us" to Salome.'

'You have been over-working that poor female brain of yours,' he said sarcastically.

'I am simply putting two and two together,' she retorted, and moved towards her boudoir-table, where the morning sun was reflected in the copper bowl containing her pot-pourri. Idly, her forefinger stirred the dried rose petals. They were almost ready to be mixed with the spices and the scented oils. She turned suddenly to face him. 'William, henceforth you and I must live together, amiably and courteously. Tell me that you would never have allowed Patience to be hanged...that first time.'

His answering look chilled her heart. 'I would,' he said, 'if it had been the only way to protect my own.'

'You would go to the lengths of sacrificing a fellow human being, and a family connection of your mother's to boot, merely to shield your brother?'

He strode towards her, his mouth twisted in fury at her stubborn incomprehension, eyes blazing with an angry fervour. She stepped back as he thrust his face towards hers. '*Merely* my brother, do you say? Are you so stupid, ma'am, as to think that any *outsider* is more precious to me than my own immediate family? Why do you think I arranged all that elaborate pretence to save the woman? I did it, my poor, witless wench, to protect you and the child you carried.'

'So,' she said, her voice low and

trembling, 'it is true. Patience spoke the truth from the pulpit. She would have gone to her death had I shown myself to be a woman completely devoid of all human feeling.'

He could not hold her glance and turned away, wishing that he could make her understand what got into a man when the honour of his family was at stake. Useless to try and convince her that he had never expected the death sentence to be passed upon Patience in the first place—how was he to read the mind of an idiot judge?—and that even it if had been necessary to place before the justices the matter of the necklace, he had anticipated transportation to be the predictable result. He clenched his fists, nails biting into the flesh of his palms. Damn my no-good, whoring brothers. Silently, he cursed them for their ceaseless escapades, and for their constant reliance upon him to get them out of trouble.

Clarissa sensed the struggle that was going on inside him, but she was untiring in her pursuit of the one small spark of goodness which she knew to be there, buried deep under the surface of family pride and innate instinct for possession.

'Cornelius was an evil man, William. You gave your protection to a monster.'

She saw a wry smile cross his face as he fidgeted about her bedroom, a male uncomfortably aware of trespassing upon the territory of the female. 'According to Patience, I too am a monster.'

'So would I have thought had I stood in her place.'

'But you are not in her place, and yet you think it.'

'Why should I not, when you buy and sell human souls and are not averse to resorting to murder when your own are threatened?'

The sounds of hounds baying in the distance rescued him from her embarrassing directness and sent him hurrying to the window. 'Lambton,' he said. 'He told me he was riding to hounds this morning, and I promised to join him.'

The realisation that the spark of goodness was obdurately determined to remain buried, caused her a fierce pang of regret, but she did not give up hope that she might be able to resurrect it if she was possessed of enough patience to stay the course. Clarissa was nothing if not optimistic. 'Shall you bring the Lambtons back to dinner?' she asked.

'Of course.' He looked surprised. 'We went to his place last time.'

'I thought...' she began tentatively, and almost faltered before the bland look of inquiry on his face. 'It was only this morning that Patience was...will there not be some awkwardness, and with the family still in mourning for Cornelius...and what Patience said about you...' She blundered to a stop.

'My friends,' he said, with slow and careful emphasis on each word, 'are not likely to believe the accusations of a jealous and demented woman.'

'No,' she agreed, 'such persons can never be relied on to tell the truth.'

He frowned, searching her face for signs that she was mocking him, but her expression was half-pleading, half-placatory, and he dimly perceived that she had decided to live in peace with something she could not change.

He nodded approvingly, as he would to a dog which he had successfully brought to heel after a long and difficult period of training. 'Quite so.' He made for the door and paused with his hand on the knob. 'Patience may lie in the churchyard,' he said, 'though not in that part that is consecrated. She may be laid to rest under the elm tree which marks the boundary.'

'Yes, William.'

Having asserted his dominion over his living chattel, William was prepared to be generous. 'She shall have a stone to mark the place with her name carved upon it.'

'Should not her father be informed of what has happened to her?' Clarissa asked. 'He cannot have heard from her for a long time.'

'I shall write to him,' William replied, 'but I am of the opinion that he will want nothing to do with the wretched business. He will be quite content to leave her body here in Piddingfold.'

'What of her husband?' Clarissa wondered.

William shrugged. 'Most like he is happy to be relieved of the burden of caring for her, and as I have no idea where he is presently residing I can do little in that quarter.'

'Whoever would have thought,' remarked his wife carefully, 'that Patience would turn out to be such a troublesome creature?'

William held her steady regard for an instant before smiling brightly. 'Do not overtax yourself today,' he advised. 'You know what Dr Anderson said about taking things very slowly during the first six months of pregnancy.'

'I will be calm,' she promised.

When her husband had gone, Clarissa walked to the window. The baying of the hounds was louder now, and she thought she could discern a flicker of movement beyond the oaks fringing the five-acre field. She spared a thought for Aunt Charlotte, not yet quite recovered from a seizure, brought on more by the discovery of Cornelius's villainy than by the manner of his death. She said aloud, 'I have buried my conscience as deep as his spark of goodness. For the sake of my children, God help me to endure...'